# The Other Side of the Coin

Wendy Mason

Grosvenor House
Publishing Limited

The right of Wendy Mason to be identified as the author of this
work has been asserted in accordance with Section 78
of the Copyright, Designs and Patents Act 1988

The book cover is copyright to Wendy Mason

This book is published by
Grosvenor House Publishing Ltd
Link House
140 The Broadway, Tolworth, Surrey, KT6 7HT.
www.grosvenorhousepublishing.co.uk

This book is a work of fiction. Any resemblance to
people or events, past or present, is purely coincidental.

A CIP record for this book
is available from the British Library

ISBN 978-1-83975-690-0

# By the same author

St Francis – An Instrument of Peace (Novum: 2018).

Not Exactly Chaucer (Conrad Press: 2020).

I dedicate this book to my wonderful husband, Harold; my two adorable grandsons, Hector and Arthur; my daughter, Rachael and her husband Dan.

# Chapter One

Maureen lay in her bed, paralysed by fear. She quelled her breath and listened for a sound. Any sound. All she could hear was the pounding of her heart.

She opened her eyes to inky-black darkness. After a few seconds, her eyes adjusted and she could make out the slight gap between the bottom of the blind and the window sill, sufficient to allow a weak sliver of moonshine to penetrate. The shadows cast by the light danced around the room, ignited her imagination and inflamed her terror. The roaring in her ears grew louder.

Her throat was as dry as parchment. She sat up, reached for a glass of water from the bedside table and drank greedily before she sank back onto her pillow and closed her eyes. Total darkness restored, she concentrated, not wishing to miss a sound, intent on identifying what it was that had caused her to wake.

There! Muffled voices.

Maureen opened her eyes and focused on locating the source. A soft murmur seeped through the dividing wall. With her ear pressed up against the Laura Ashley wallpaper, Maureen could just make out a woman's voice; quiet, cold and accusing. Beth's voice.

A much deeper male voice rumbled indistinctly.

Beth spoke again, much more urgently. Clearer. She seemed to be pleading with her partner, her words interspersed with hiccupping sobs.

A thud, followed by a sharp cry.

So, this was what had woken her: the unmistakable sounds of domestic violence.

It was a common enough event. She knew, from reading the newspapers, that this scene was being re-enacted across the country in countless homes. But what should she do? How did other people react? Or, didn't they? Why didn't she simply turn over, go back to sleep and forget the whole thing?

She couldn't turn a blind eye to this. Not this time. It was happening here, in Emilia Boulevard, quite literally on her doorstep. And it was happening to Beth, the young mother she had recently befriended.

But what to do? Should she bang on the wall and alert her neighbour to the fact that she knew his grubby little secret? Should she wait until Beth's partner was out and confront her with the truth – *no matter how sorry he says he is, it will happen again. Believe me, I know*. Should she alert the Police or Social Services? After all, a child was involved; Beth's young son was in the house with them and, unless he was mercifully asleep, he would probably hear everything that was happening. What impact would that have on him in later years? What if the child was being abused – physically, or in other ways?

Maureen breathed in deeply through her nose, then exhaled slowly through her mouth. She repeated the process. Air entered her lungs but somehow appeared to be starved of oxygen. She tried again. No better. She threw back her duvet, reached over and pushed up the blind, opened the window and gulped in the cool fresh air.

In the distance, she could hear the gentle lapping of the waves, which helped to create the sensation of floating and calmed her nerves. The sound of the sea had been the deciding factor when she and Giles had chosen to make this house their home. She would have preferred a sea view, but their budget wouldn't stretch that far and, after all, they were only just around the corner from the beach. For the past thirty-five years, the sound of the breaking waves had been her constant companion. It had soothed her as she nursed their only child, Anna, who'd been a fretful baby from the day she was born. Five years later, it had also been her comfort as she nursed Giles through those few painful months until he died from pancreatic cancer at the ridiculously young age of thirty-eight.

An owl hooted.

Maureen picked up her mobile and checked the time. Three o'clock. Too late, or was that too early to do anything now? Tomorrow morning she'd call in on Beth and try to persuade her to seek help. She had to do something. She didn't want to think that Beth might become another statistic. She could see the headlines in the *West Briton* – *Young Falmouth mother dies at the hand of her partner. Neighbours heard her cries for help but did nothing.*

On the other hand, she knew that by speaking up, she risked being cast in the role of a nosy busybody. But then, she'd mistakenly allowed that to stop her in the past. This time she had no choice.

Emilia Boulevard was a quiet and narrow street, consisting of Edwardian terraced houses, flanked on one side by the hotels and apartment blocks on Cliff

Road and on the other by Melville Road and the Falmouth Docks to Truro branch line. The south-facing front gardens rose steeply from the pavement. Some owners had nibbled into the bank and excavated tons of soil to create an off-road parking space. Maureen had kept Giles's ancient green Morris Minor Traveller, but she didn't really enjoy driving and was quite happy leaving it parked on the road outside her front gate. She kept it taxed and MOT'd but rarely used it, especially since she'd received her bus pass and discovered a local grocery shop that provided home deliveries.

Instead, Maureen had landscaped their front garden to create picturesque tiers of planting spaces for small oases of specimen trees, shrubs and flowers. She was particularly pleased with her banana tree, the Cornish palm and her selection of camellia, now covered in buds and even a few flowers, some two-tone pink, some white. As she walked down her path, she noticed that the daffodils were budding and would soon be trumpeting in triumph. She loved these simple, fragrant symbols of the forthcoming spring.

The neighbouring garden, which now occupied Maureen's immediate attention, could only be described as ugly. She held onto the cast iron handrail and clambered up the concrete steps that rose from the wooden gate to the front door. On either side of her, crazy-paving was organised in layers, dressed with occasional pots containing dead plants and tufts of grass. A scooter, with its front wheel missing, had been abandoned beside the steps, a deflated football lay discarded by the front door, and a dead Christmas tree, devoid of needles, stood propped against the fence.

Reaching the front door, she peered over her glasses trying to read the names on the doorbells. Four flats in a house the same size as her own. How did they all squeeze in? Most of the writing was faded, indecipherable, and in any case, she realised now that she didn't know Beth's family name. She'd never visited Beth at home before; they always met up for a coffee in the café under the railway bridge. Their very first meeting had come about during a particularly heavy downpour in early January. Maureen, Beth and Harrison had, quite literally, bumped into each other on the pavement outside the cafe.

The rain was pouring down and the wind had howled around her, making the umbrella impossible to manage. She collapsed it down, stuffed it into her shoulder bag and quickened her pace. That morning's relaxing head massage, trim and blow dry was a thing of the past, and her sleek grey bob was now a soggy mess. Her fringe lay plastered to her forehead. Rain dripped down her neck. Thank goodness she hadn't succumbed to a perm. By now she'd have looked like one of those woollen pompoms she used to make for Anna when she was a baby. She could never understand why many of her age group resorted to short perms as soon as they reached their sixties. So ageing. This style gave her confidence. She'd been told it made her look much younger than her sixty-five years; although, on reflection, it was probably her hairdresser who'd paid her that particular compliment.

She needed a coffee and decided to treat herself to one in that new place she'd been meaning to try. She could wait there in comfort for the worst of this squall to pass. Head down, she rushed towards the café entrance and collided with a small child coming from the opposite direction. His mother, who Maureen guessed would be in her early twenties, stood behind him with her hand on his shoulder.

'Let the lady in first, buddy,' she said.

'I wet.' The little boy laughed.

'I think we all are.' Maureen opened the door. 'Let's go in and get these coats off, shall we?'

She led the boy and his mother into the warm cosiness of the American-styled diner. The smell of coffee made her tummy rumble. Her hair appointment had meant an early start, too early for her usual bowl of porridge. She noticed a plate of chocolate chip cookies on the counter covered with a glass dome. She decided to indulge – why not? After all, she was still the well-proportioned Size 14 she'd been on her wedding day.

Maureen wasn't quite sure how they all managed to be seated together. The fact that they'd stumbled through the door, shrugged off their sodden coats, hung them on the coat stand and then turned to the waiter as one, obviously convinced him that he was looking at a family group. He offered them the window seat, manoeuvred a child's high chair into place, and handed around menus. He helped the young boy to climb up, fastened the safety straps around him and then waited to take their order.

'I'll take a flat white coffee and a chocolate chip cookie, please,' Maureen said, handing back her menu.

'Double shot espresso, please. And what about you, buddy?'

'Milkshake, please.'

'A vanilla milkshake and a cookie for my son, please.'

Maureen smiled at the young boy. 'I'm Maureen. What's your name?'

'Harry.'

Maureen's heart thudded and her fingers tingled. Harry! What a coincidence.

'That's a lovely name,' she said.

'It's Harrison really, but he can't manage that yet. But then, he's only two and a half.' The woman reached over and ruffled his blond hair. 'And I'm Beth.'

'I recognise you both. Don't you live in one of the flats next door to me? I'm at Number 32 Emilia Boulevard.'

The young mother nodded and looked out of the window. 'It's hentin' it down out there.'

'Henting?'

'Pourin' down,' Beth laughed. 'You're not from Cornwall then?'

'My husband and I moved here from London, thirty-five years ago. With his job.'

'What's he do?'

'He was an accountant.'

'Was?'

'Giles died thirty years ago.'

Beth's eyes widened. 'I'm so sorry.' She reached across the table and patted Maureen's hand gently.

Maureen looked at Beth. Her short black hair was cut into what Maureen had heard described as a pixie cut. It emphasised her dark brown eyes, which were framed by long, thick eyelashes. Her face had no trace of make-up. Not that she needed any; her complexion was to die for. Maureen never left the house without her foundation, powder and red lippy. She smiled at Beth and then turned her attention back to the waiter as he delivered their order.

'Mm, Harrison, my cookie is amazing. What do you think?'

'Good.' Harrison put his biscuit on his plate and stuck up his two thumbs.

The two women laughed.

Since that first meeting, coffee mornings had become a weekly event – every Wednesday at eleven for coffee, milkshake, cookies, and Maureen's fix of therapeutic cuddles from Harrison.

Maureen paused on the doorstep, wondering whether interfering in her neighbour's personal life might impact on their relationship. Then she thought about Harrison, witnessing all that abuse, and she scanned the four doorbells again.

Beth had mentioned that they lived in a duplex apartment on the ground and first floor. Maureen decided to try Flat No. 1. She pressed the button. Nothing happened. Maureen peered through the patterned glass panel in the door. No one. She knocked on the wooden panel. This appeared to have the desired effect. She could hear the tap, tap, tap of footsteps.

The door opened.

'Maureen. Alright?'

'I'm good, thanks.'

Beth stood back from the door, opening it wide. 'Come in. Want some coffee?'

Maureen stepped into the hall. 'Coffee sounds good, thanks.'

She glanced around. Four piles of mail were stacked across the bottom step of the staircase. Hung from a coat hook, a large plastic recycling bag overflowed with empty wine bottles and beer cans. A second bag spilled over with newspapers, advertising flyers and discarded envelopes. A large padlock and chain secured an old-fashioned black bike to the radiator. The hall smelt musty; a mixture of damp washing and mouldy wallpaper.

She followed Beth into her small, cluttered kitchen. Dirty pots were sprawled across the draining board. A loaf of bread lay on its side, the bag open to the elements. The pedal bin overflowed and smelt of dirty nappies.

'Take a seat.' Beth removed a pile of papers from the stool. 'Sorry about the doorbell. I took the battery out so it don't wake Harrison.'

'Where is he?' Maureen asked as she perched on the seat at the small pine dining table.

'Just took him up for his nap. He'll probably sleep for an hour. Dearovim.'

Maureen swallowed her disappointment; a cuddle from Harrison always gave her a rush of affection. She thought she may well be addicted to his hugs. It would have also helped to strengthen her quickly diminishing courage and resolve.

Beth switched on the kettle, took two mugs from the cupboard, spooned in a teaspoon of instant coffee and poured on the boiling water. 'Milk and one sugar, right?'

Maureen nodded. 'I've brought him some cookies. I baked them this morning.' She reached into her shoulder bag, pulled out a small package of tin foil and put it on the table.

'Thanks. He'll enjoy them.'

Maureen picked up her mug and took a sip. 'Beth… I'm not sure how to say this, but…the truth is that the walls on these houses are quite thin.'

Beth put her mug down on the kitchen counter. 'You mean you were earwiggin' on us arguin' last night?' Her voice was frosty.

'Mm. I know it's nothing to do with me, and I don't want to interfere, but...well, do you think you should get some help? Some counselling or something?'

'You're right.'

Maureen took a deep breath as the tight band of tension in her chest relaxed.

'It's *nowt* to do with you!' Beth's normally beautiful cupid lips curled into a snarl.

'Oh, Beth, I'm sorry. Please don't be angry with me. It's just that I'm so worried about you.'

'You'd better leave. Now! Steve'll be back any minute. He won't be happy to know you've been round stickin' your bleddy nose in where it's not wanted.'

Maureen put her mug on the table and stood. 'Beth, please forgive me. I only want to help. It can't be good for Harrison to hear all these arguments. And just look at your arms, they're covered in bruises. What would happen if the police were called? Or Social Services?'

Beth tugged at her sleeves in a futile attempt to cover the black and blue fingerprints. She glared at Maureen. 'Leave! Now!'

'Okay, I'm going. But if you need me, I'm only next door.' Maureen moved to the kitchen door and turned back to face Beth. 'You've got my number. Call me. Anytime.'

Back from her morning of shopping, Maureen stirred her coffee and fiddled with the daffodils in front of her, turning some of the opening trumpets to face outwards to fashion the bunch into a more pleasing dome shape.

The perfume wafted over her. To find any space in Maureen's life, flowers had to be natural. None of this hothouse, dyed nonsense with no fragrance sold on garage forecourts. She'd been enjoying bunches of cut daffodils for weeks now. Their early availability always came as a surprise to her. She'd purchased her first bunch three weeks before Christmas from the man on the pier. Her blue and white jug on the kitchen table had been replenished weekly ever since.

She'd spent the past three days and much of the nights, worrying about Beth, and especially Harrison. Wondering what, if anything, she should do. She was no nearer to making a decision. Should she toss a coin?

What would Giles have said? Knowing him, he'd have said: *'Drop it, Maureen. You've done your bit.'*

Or Anna, what would she say? *'Mum, you simply have to do something. You know how this could end. You can't give up after one knockback. Where's your resilience?'*

Good question.

Gulping down the last of her coffee, she loaded her cup and saucer into the dishwasher and walked through into the hall. Lifting the lid of the dark-oak monk's settle, she picked out a pair of her sturdy walking shoes and then reached inside the stair cupboard for her winter coat and a cream woolly scarf.

Her heart pounded as she knocked on Beth's front door for only the second time ever. A large figure loomed behind the delicate stained-glass panels. The door swung open to reveal Steve; Beth's partner. He was a huge bear of a man – about six-foot-two, she guessed, and getting on for twenty stone – but not fat. All muscle. His shoulders were enormous. She almost lost her nerve but knew that to turn and run would solve nothing.

'I've come to see Beth,' she gulped and tried to control her breathing.

'Come in.' He smiled and opened the door wide. 'It's Maureen isn't it?'

Maureen followed him into the kitchen. It looked much tidier than earlier in the week. No dirty pots stacked in the sink. The piles of papers had been tidied away. The pine dining table was clear, clean and smelt of wood polish.

'Can I get you a tea or coffee?'

'No, thank you. I can't stop, I just wanted to invite Beth and Harrison over for tea.'

Steve seemed to crumple before her eyes. 'She's not here anymore, the thing is...' He sank onto a stool and put his head in his hands. Two enormous tears squeezed through his fingers and rolled down his chin. 'She's left me.' He wiped the tears away with the back of his hands, but they were replaced with a steady stream of fresh ones.

Maureen sat down on the stool opposite him. She hated it when men cried. It hadn't happened to her very often, but in moments like this, she always struggled to find the right words to say. *Serves you right for knocking her about* didn't appear quite appropriate right now. She wanted to put her arm over his shoulder and give him a hug, but that didn't seem very appropriate either.

'What happened?' She reached into her coat pocket, found a small packet of tissues, and placed them on the table in front of him.

He took a couple, wiped away his tears and blew his nose, sniffed and looked across at Maureen.

'She told me you'd been round to see her, and that you heard us arguing. She was worried that you might contact Social Services and she could lose custody of Harrison. She adores that boy. He's her life. She said she couldn't take the risk, packed her bags and moved out.'

'Where is she?'

'She wouldn't tell me where they were going. She said it wasn't safe for her to have anything more to do with me.' He reached for another tissue. 'I'm going to miss her so much. Both of them.'

'But if you felt like that about her, why-'

'Why did I knock her about?' Steve rubbed his hand through his hair and looked Maureen in the eye. 'Maureen, you have to believe me, I'd never hurt a hair on her head. I love that girl.' His eyes were wide, pleading, and glistening with unshed tears.

She wanted to believe him, but then remembered the last time she'd seen Beth. 'But I saw the bruises.'

'They were from where I caught hold of her arms to stop her. She was attacking me. She's the violent one.'

'Really? I can't believe Beth could be violent. She seems so patient with Harrison, and she's such a slip of a thing. How could she possibly abuse you?'

'It always happens when she has a drink. A couple of glasses of wine and she'll suddenly pick an argument and start punching.'

'I know we've only recently become friends, but I've grown so fond of Harrison.' Maureen twisted her hands together as she realised that this was a complete understatement. She thought about Harrison all the time, wished the hours away until the next time she saw him, craved for the next cuddle. She looked up and noticed Steve was watching her. 'And Beth, of course,' she said. 'I want to help them both if I can. Surely you must have some idea of where she could be?'

Steve shook his head slowly.

'Has she got family? Could she have gone to them?'

'Her mother. But they don't get on. She lives somewhere near Bodmin.'

'What's her family name?'

'Her mother's name is Rowe. But Beth was married to Harrison's father. His name is Taylor, Reg, or Ron or something like that. Beth's hardly seen him since he moved out when the kid was only a few months old, but she kept his name. He's in the forces, or at least he was. The navy I think.'

'What about friends? Could she have gone to stay with someone?'

'There's a school friend she'd see now and then. Jan. She lives in Truro, but I don't know any contact details.'

Maureen scrambled to her feet. She smiled at Steve, moved around the table and patted his arm. 'I don't suppose you've reported her missing to the police?'

'That's the last thing she'd want. Anyway, I'm sure they wouldn't be interested. She's not missing. Just gone.'

'You're probably right.' Maureen sighed. 'Don't get up, Steve. I'll see myself out.'

She glanced back at him as she reached the kitchen door. He had his head in his hands once more. His enormous shoulders shook with what appeared to be genuine emotion.

She entered the hall and crossed the cream and burgundy tiled floor. She'd been concerned for Beth and

Harrison when she'd arrived on the front doorstep. But now, as she left, she was even more worried about Harrison's safety. Were they now homeless, sleeping in a shop doorway somewhere? How would such a young boy cope with that sort of existence? And, if she was to believe Steve, she'd clearly misjudged Beth. Could she really be violent? Was Harrison even more at risk because she'd interfered? God, she would never forgive herself if something happened to him.

# Chapter Two

Maureen's pulse rate increased noticeably as the receptionist, who'd warmly introduced herself as Sally, ushered her into the manager's office. The plaque on the door read: Manager, Ms P Andrews.

Ms P Andrews sat in a green leather swivel chair behind a mahogany desk, turning the blotting paper pages of a leather file and signing letters with an expensive-looking fountain pen. She looked up as Maureen was shown in and stood to greet her. 'Do take a seat.' She waved at the chair positioned strategically opposite hers.

As they both sat, Maureen noticed that although they were about the same height, her seat was lower. She shuffled in her chair, aware of feeling intimidated, and annoyed because she knew that was the intention.

Maureen guessed the woman was in her late thirties. She wore a smart black suit and mauve blouse, and her hair was tied back in a bun. Her make-up was minimal and well applied, her voice warm and soothing. Maureen wondered what the P stood for: Petunia? Penny? Patricia?

'Would you like a cup of tea or coffee?'

'Tea would be lovely. White, one sugar, thank you.'

'I'll just go and get that organised myself. I don't want to take Sally away from reception.' Ms P's voice dropped to a whisper. 'We may get an unwanted visitor.'

She opened her file, took out a slim booklet and pushed it across the desk. 'Would you like to look through our brochure while I'm gone?' She left the room without waiting for a reply.

Maureen leafed through the pamphlet. It contained pictures of the gardens, filled with shrubs and flower beds and surrounded on three sides by a tall stone wall. The internal images on the next few pages included the reception and main hall, with its majestic curved staircase, and a large kitchen with a central dining table surrounded by a mixture of chairs. There was a wide-angled shot of the lounge with dark blue, comfortable-looking sofas and armchairs, and a large, wall-mounted TV. There were also pictures of a small classroom and a crèche with images of two children playing in a plastic sandpit while another three sat painting at a large table. The photographs were taken from behind the children, ensuring they could not be identified.

This was more like a four-star hotel than a refuge hostel for women. The glossy leaflet portrayed the benefits of staying here but was obviously intended for marketing to prospective benefactors, rather than potential customers.

What on earth was she doing here? She'd never even heard of this place until she'd spoken to Mrs Rowe. She'd spent the past few nights tossing and turning, consumed with worry over Beth and Harrison: terrified that she'd never see Harrison again, wondering how genuine Steve was and if his tears were simply an act to distract her from the truth. Was it somehow her fault, as he had implied? Had Beth fled because she was frightened Maureen would report them to Social

Services? Had Steve beaten Beth, and she'd run away in terror? Perhaps he'd killed her in anger and hidden her body somewhere. In which case, where was Harrison? Her heart ached with the dread of it all.

In the early hours of the morning, Maureen had made up her mind to trace them. Perhaps she could put Beth's mind at rest: re-assure her that she had no intention of reporting her to Social Services. She would offer to help in any way possible and ensure that they could resume their friendship. She could not, would not imagine a future without Harrison.

After breakfast, as soon as the library opened, she'd visited and copied down all the entries for the name *Rowe* from the Bodmin area telephone directory. She was unsuccessful with her first three calls but hit lucky on the fourth.

'I'm sorry to bother you, but I'm trying to find Mrs Rowe, mother of Beth and grandmother to Harrison?'

'What's she done this time?'

Maureen faltered. 'I'm Maureen James – her neighbour in Falmouth. I'm concerned about them both. They went missing last week and I'm trying to trace them.'

'No use asking me, she won't tell me nowt. Knows she'll get short shrift. Dafter than a buzza that one. Don't worry about her. She'll come up smelling of roses. Always does.'

'I understand she has an old school friend in Truro called Jan?'

'Aye, they be good friends. Always minching off school together. She could be at Jan's.'

'Do you have Jan's address?'

'Backalong, but not now. Last I 'eard she were working the taxis in Truro. Good girl, Jan. Sensible 'ead on 'er shoulders, unlike Beth.'

Maureen flinched. 'Mrs Rowe, you and your daughter may have some issues, but I simply want to help Beth and Harrison. And to do that I need to find them.' Maureen struggled to keep the frustration from her voice. 'Do you have *any* idea where she could be?'

'She may be back to St Mary's.'

'St Mary's?'

'Refuge in Truro, back of the Cathedral. That's where she went when she split with that 'usband of 'ers. Her caseworker got 'er that flat in Falmouth. I thought she were in clover but, no, she 'ad to ask that gorilla, Steve, to move in. Can't stand being alone that one. Should know better by now.'

Mrs Rowe provided Maureen with the number for St Mary's refuge and Maureen ended the call, wondering how any mother could seem so disinterested in the whereabouts of her child and grandson.

'Here we are.' Ms P pushed the door open with her trim bottom and placed a silver tray with two bone china teacups and a plate of biscuits onto the desk. 'Do help yourself. I managed to find some chocolate digestives. Now, what can I do for you? Sally said something about you wanting to donate?'

'My neighbour, Beth Taylor, and her son, Harrison, stayed here last year. She told me how you rely almost entirely on charitable donations since the council cuts kicked in.'

'Please forgive me, Mrs James, but data protection prevents me from acknowledging, or denying, that Beth was ever a guest here.'

Maureen stirred her tea and picked up a biscuit. 'I completely understand. But either way, she told me what a wonderful job you do here, helping the mothers find work, looking after the children in the crèche while they undergo training, go out to work, or pursue longer-term housing options. It sounded impressive, and I wondered if I could have a look around?'

Maureen was quite proud of how much she'd managed to pick up about how the refuge functioned from that quick look through the leaflet.

Ms P frowned and glanced at her watch. 'I could give you a quick tour. Most of our ladies are either out at work or in the classroom.'

Maureen gulped down her tea, put the remnants of her half-eaten biscuit in her saucer and followed Ms P.

Ms P led Maureen back into the hall and opened the first door they came to. 'This is our kitchen/diner. The mums take it in turn to cook dinner, which is always at five-thirty, so we can all eat together with the children.' She crossed the hall and opened the next door. 'This is the lounge.' She stepped back to give Maureen a view of the room. 'Along here is our classroom. Some of our ladies are in class right now, so I hope you understand that, for privacy reasons, I won't be able to take you in, but I could show you our crèche, as long as you don't take any photos.'

Maureen glanced around the room. Seven children sat on a fluffy green rug; three girls, four boys. None of them even vaguely resembled Harrison. A young woman sat on a three-legged stool telling them a story. She looked up as they entered.

'Good morning, Ms Andrews. Children, say good morning to our visitor.'

'Good morning,' the youngsters chorused.

'Hello. Sorry to interrupt.' Maureen smiled at the children. 'Please carry on with your story.' She felt forlorn. Of course, she should have known that finding Beth and Harrison wasn't going to be easy, but she had hoped…oh well.

Ms P led Maureen back to reception, where Sally stood by her desk. She held up the phone, her hand over the mouthpiece.

'Prudence…Councillor Evans. He wants a word.'

Ms P turned around to face Maureen. 'I have to take this. Sorry.'

Maureen realised that she was being dismissed. She reached into her shoulder bag and pulled out an envelope. 'I think you're doing a wonderful job here. Please accept this donation, and thank you for your time.'

Ms P took the offering with one hand and shook Maureen's hand with the other. 'Thank you so much. We are always grateful for any financial support. As you can see, your contribution will go to a good cause.'

She turned her back on Maureen and took the phone from Sally. 'Councillor, so good to hear from you,' she purred.

Maureen opened the front door and hurried out, closing it firmly behind her. She wanted to be out of sight before Ms P – or Prudence as she now knew her to be – opened the envelope and discovered the cheque was only for £50. Somehow, Maureen knew she'd be disappointed.

On reflection, perhaps it should have been more. After all, she could afford it. Giles had left her with a healthy pension and a life insurance policy sufficient to pay off the mortgage. She also had her state pension now, but she was always cautious with money, frightened of these scams and sucker letters she'd heard so much about. She'd not included her address on either the cheque or the envelope, just to be sure that the hostel couldn't hound her for more. Maybe she'd send another cheque at Christmas.

The unsuccessful visit to St Mary's, and the niggling guilt over the size of her donation, caused Maureen's mood to dip. She decided to improve the situation with a visit to the food hall in Marks and Spencer. A small fillet steak, asparagus and fresh garden peas for her dinner, a fruit pot to enjoy on her porridge the next morning, and some sliced ham, tomatoes and fresh bread – still warm from the oven – for lunch when she got home.

She clutched her shopping bag and wandered back across the piazza, pausing to watch a few toddlers on the small roundabout. Realising quickly that Harrison wasn't one of them, she moved on, rounded the corner and was relieved to see a taxi.

'Could you take me to the train station, please?'

'Hop in.' The driver switched on the meter, which immediately registered the minimum fare of £3.20.

As the taxi pulled away, Maureen leaned forward. 'I don't suppose you know anyone called Jan who works in Truro as a taxi driver? She must be in her early twenties.'

'Can't say I do. Why?'

'She's a friend of my ex-neighbours, a girl called Beth, and her young son, Harrison. I'm trying to contact them both.'

He gave her one of his taxi cards and a biro. 'Here, write your details on the back and I'll ask around.'

'That's so kind of you, thanks.' She wrote down her name and address, added her telephone number and handed it back to him.

He pulled into the station's taxi rank, switched off his engine and turned to face her. 'That's £5.40, my dear.'

She handed over £6, told him to keep the change and hurried into the booking hall. Glancing up at the electronic timetable, she discovered that the next train to Falmouth was due to leave in five minutes. She walked quickly down the platform, clambered into the first carriage, found a forward-facing seat and sank into it.

Thank goodness she didn't need to wait for a train. The platforms appeared to enjoy a unique micro-climate; they were always much colder than the rest of Truro.

She was tired. All these sleepless nights, plus the excitement of this morning's trip, had taken its toll. The train pulled out of the station and swayed rhythmically. Her head nodded, and suddenly, Anna was with her.

'Mummy, Mummy, look!'

'What darling? What am I looking at?'

'The rabbit. Look! Over there!'

A lone rabbit, frightened by the noise of the train, raced across the field beside them and disappeared into a small copse of trees. Anna must have been almost five at the time. They'd been into Truro to purchase her first school uniform; such a happy time. Only two months later, her life would be turned upside down when Giles was diagnosed with pancreatic cancer. Maureen's eyes filled with tears as she remembered how the consultant had given them the prognosis. He'd advised Giles to put his affairs in order and dropped the bombshell – he probably had six months to live. As it turned out, it was only four.

'Tickets please.'

Maureen fumbled in her bag for her purse, removed the return ticket and her railcard and held them up for inspection.

'Thank you.' The woman took her ticket and stamped it. 'You look after yourself, dear. Looks like you're going down with a cold.'

'I'm fine, thanks.'

But Maureen knew she was anything but fine.

It was a sheer indulgence. It wasn't that cold, especially for February, but Maureen had a yearning to be snuggled up in the armchair, wrapped in a blanket, enjoying a mug of hot chocolate as she relaxed beside a roaring log fire. She picked up an old copy of the *West Briton* and ripped off a sheet.

This fireplace was the first thing she and Giles installed after they bought the house. The previous owners had unbelievably ripped out the original and installed an ugly, wall-mounted electric contraption. She and Giles had spent weeks touring the salvage yards and auctions until they eventually discovered this one in a house clearance warehouse tucked away at the back of Penryn.

'Look there.' Maureen had pointed to the sign. 'They may have something. Can we try?'

Giles turned the Morris around and pulled onto the small visitor car park. 'It looks a bit scruffy. Are you sure?'

In answer, Maureen clambered out and waited for him to join her at the front entrance. 'Come on, it looks really promising.'

They wandered through the shop, meandering past antique chairs, wardrobes and desks. The proprietor responded to their question by directing them outside to a rear yard.

Water troughs and old chimney pots of various sizes were arranged around the edge of the courtyard. Wrought iron gates leaned against the walls. And there, centre stage, was the most wonderful fireplace. Not only did it have the wooden classical columns and double mantle shelf, but also black tiles on either side of the fire grate, decorated with stylised tulips similar to those in the glass panels of their front door. When they'd first viewed their house, the estate agent had told them proudly that the door panel flowers were a feature attributed to Charles Vosey. They'd tried to look impressed, not wishing to show their ignorance; neither of them had a clue at the time that Vosey was a famous architect and interior designer.

As soon as she spotted the fireplace, she knew she had to have it. Giles bartered the proprietor down to an affordable price, who even agreed to deliver it and, for a reasonable amount, to install it for them. Giles was never any good at the practical DIY work around the home, although he had carefully rubbed down the wood and painted it to perfection. She still had some happy times to remember him by.

She ripped off a few more pages and twisted each sheet to make spills, stacked them, added kindling sticks and a small log. She lit the paper and blew gently on the flame until the twigs began to crackle and the log started to scorch. It was well worth the effort, even if just for the comforting smell.

Tidying up the remnants of the newspaper, she noticed the page with personal announcements. Someone had offered a small reward for the return of a purse lost somewhere near the Hall for Cornwall Theatre in Truro. Another was searching for the much-loved family cat, black with green eyes, missing from the Kea area. One woman was looking for a male companion, sixty to seventy-years-old, for meals out, theatre visits and walking trips. Perhaps she could place an advert to encourage Beth to contact her?

By now, the fire was well lit. She added a few more logs and retreated into the kitchen to make her drink and mull over the wording she should use. Something not too desperate; it needed to be light and encouraging. But most of all, it needed to work. Whatever it took.

# Chapter Three

Beth looked up from reading the newspaper as Jan's mobile trilled.

'Hi Nick, what's up?' Jan listened. 'What do you mean, an *old biddy*? I hope you didn't go giving out my contact details to some stranger?' Jan reached into her handbag and pulled out a pen and notepad. 'Good. Okay, give me her number.'

Beth watched Jan as she finished the call and stuffed her mobile into the back pocket of her jeans. 'Problems?' Beth asked as she glanced down at Harrison. He was fast asleep beside her, his fluffy rabbit and blanket clutched tightly.

'That was a colleague. Nick. He's just had your neighbour, Maureen James, in his cab asking about me. Steve must have told her we were friends.'

Beth shook her head. 'He doesn't know you're a taxi driver.'

'Perhaps Steve contacted your mum?'

'More likely Maureen did. She scared me shitless when she came around last week. I thought for sure she'd contact Social Services.' Beth looked down at her sleeping son. 'I'd die if I lost him.'

Jan sighed. 'You're so impetuous. Why don't you press pause and think sometimes? Social Services know you're a good mum. They'd do anything to help you.'

'But what if they spoke to Steve? He could lie. He was gutted when I told him I were off. He could say owt, just to get back at me.' Beth burst into tears.

Jan reached into her pocket, pulled out a small pack of tissues and handed a couple to Beth. 'Oh dear, Beth. You had everything going for you. Nice flat, good location for Harrison, a fresh start. Why on earth did you have to get mixed up with him?'

'Loneliness, I guess.'

'But why choose someone who's violent?'

Beth shrugged.

'You certainly know how to pick 'em.' Jan stood and collected up the empty coffee mugs. 'I'd better go. My shift starts soon. Don't answer the door while I'm out. Ring if you need me.'

Beth glanced up from the property pages of the *West Briton*. 'I didn't hear you come in last night.'

'No, it was after midnight. You were both fast asleep.'

Beth watched as Jan shaped the bright orange Play-Doh and put her completed effort on the coffee table.

'Here you go, Harrison.'

'Duck.'

'Well done. It *is* a duck. Quack, quack, quack. Now you make one.' She handed him a ball of the squidgy material and sniffed her hands. 'Mm, I love the smell of this stuff. It takes me back to when we were kids.'

Beth smiled. 'You always were weird.'

'Harry do it.' Harrison put his version of a duck next to Jan's, grinned and clapped his hands together.

'That's brilliant. How many ducks do we have now?' Jan asked.

Harrison pointed at each duck in turn. 'One, two... two ducks.' He picked up his fluffy blue rabbit, climbed onto the sofa and cuddled up to his mother. 'Dummy?'

'You shouldn't need it during the day. Not now you're a big boy.'

'Dummy!' he wailed. Two big tears rolled down his cheeks. 'Dummy, Mummy. I tired.'

Beth reached into her cardigan pocket and handed the dummy to him. He popped it into his mouth, closed his eyes and was instantly asleep.

'Have you thought any more about what you're going to do?' Jan asked.

'Want me out?'

'Don't be silly. You can stay forever as far as I'm concerned, but sleeping on a blow-up mattress isn't exactly good for Harrison.'

'I know. But I can't contact my caseworker for help. If she found out I were sofa surfin' she'd have Harrison into foster care before I could blink.'

'You've still got the keys to your flat in Falmouth. You could go back when Steve's at work and get the locks changed. He's not supposed to be living there anyway, so you could always call the police if he kicked off.'

'Too late. He texted me yesterday. He's moved out and handed the keys back. Moved into a house closer to Helston, where he works. I rang my landlord first thing this mornin' but he's already re-let the flat. I tried pleadin' but he said I'd breached my contract by sub-lettin'. Demanded my keys back. Told me if I didn't get them to him within the week, he'd change all the locks and send me a bill. I'm not sure where he thinks he's going to send it. He's no idea know where I am, but

I guess he'd come after me through the courts. It seems I'm stuffed.'

'Oh, Beth!' Jan sighed.

'You sound like my bleddy mother.'

'I'd best get off. My shift starts in half an hour.' Jan picked up her keys from the coffee table. 'I'll treat us to fish and chips tonight. Be back about eight.'

Beth picked up Harrison and laid him gently on the corner of the sofa, one cushion positioned to support his head and the other placed to stop him rolling off the edge. She put the fluffy rabbit on his tummy. He never stirred. With a bit of luck, he'd nap like this for an hour or more. She picked up the newspaper and turned to the personal column. Her stomach lurched as she saw her name in bold print:

*To Beth and Harrison.*

*Please contact me. I miss the coffee, milkshake and cookie mornings with you both, and I look forward to seeing you again soon. Maureen.*

Beth sighed; Maureen had been a good friend to them both since they'd met. But why on earth would she risk getting in touch? She'd left Steve to get away from her. Anyway, there was no going back to Falmouth now – except to hand in her keys. She folded the paper over so that the personal column was on top. She'd show Jan when she got in tonight.

Beth checked that Harrison was safe, went through into the kitchen and made herself a mug of coffee. She gazed out of the kitchen window while the kettle boiled. The honey-gold triple spires of the cathedral shone in the morning sunshine. Jan had once told her that Truro was one of only three cathedrals in the UK with three spires, the others being Lichfield and one in Edinburgh. Jan was always collecting bits of useless information like that. She reckoned they were useful to pass on to her passengers and earned her extra tips.

Her stomach churned somersaults as she realised that St Mary's Refuge snuggled behind that building. She hated the thought of being forced back there. For a start, her mother would guess that's where she was and turn up, half-heartedly offering them a home. Home! That was a laugh. The last place she wanted to be. She and her mother had never got on – even less since her mother had insisted on taking Ron's side when they'd split up. Anyway, she knew full well her mother didn't really want her. She'd only offer because of some misplaced sense of duty – or guilt.

The word *refuge* conjured up thoughts of safety, peace and tranquillity. It may be a safe haven from the outside world and those that threatened you, but not from the bullying and control of that stuck up cow, Prudence Andrews. Such a bleddy snot. Harrison had only been six months old at the time they'd arrived, and Beth accepted that she may have been a young first-time mother, but she didn't need to be told how to change his nappy, how to bath him, how to live her life. She'd found it difficult to bite her tongue and stop herself from losing her temper. More like a regime than a refuge. She'd hated every minute and would do almost anything to avoid a return.

But where did that leave them? The only option had been Jan's tiny one-bedroom flat, with Beth sleeping on the sofa and Harrison on the blow-up mattress. Jan had been right: this place was definitely unsuitable. If only she hadn't lost the Falmouth flat. Jan was right about that as well. She should have changed the locks and told Steve to go. Without him there, there would be no arguments and Maureen would have had nothing to report to Social Services.

She sighed. All she'd ever wanted was to provide a nice home and a loving environment for Harrison. Why did she keep getting it so wrong? Her shoulder bag was perched on the kitchen table. She reached in, extracted a packet of paracetamol and swallowed two tablets. Perhaps she should ask Steve to forgive her, beg him to take her back. Why had she fought with him anyway? She couldn't even remember what it was about. Perhaps they could move in and share his new place? He wasn't exactly good looking, but he had sexy broad shoulders – definitely stuggy, as her mum would say.

She returned to the lounge, curled up on the sofa with Harrison and closed her eyes. If only she could catch up on her sleep, things might begin to make more sense.

Jan stood up so quickly that her knee caught on the leg of the kitchen table, which rocked and knocked over the bottle of tomato sauce.

'How can you even think about going back to him? You must be mad.'

'He's crazy about me and great with Harrison.'

'And he uses you as a punchbag. Remember?'

'He won't do it again.'

'Oh, Beth. Don't be so bloody naive.' Jan rolled up the remnants of their fish and chip supper, throwing the paper and empty boxes into the rubbish bin. 'I don't know how you manage to pick these violent men, but you must know by now, from experience if nothing else, once a man hits you, it will happen again.'

'But-'

'You did the right thing, both times. You walked away for your own sake and to protect Harrison.' Jan reached over, picked up the ketchup, wiped the lid with some paper towel and put the bottle back in the cupboard.

'I didn't leave because of Steve. Maureen were about to report me.'

'And if you go back to Steve, I'll report you.'

Beth gasped. 'You can't be serious.'

'I care about you both, Beth. I will not stand by and see you go back into a dangerous situation like that.' Jan filled the kettle and switched it on. 'Look, you've just shown me the advert Maureen's placed. If she's gone to all that trouble, then she obviously wants to help. Perhaps she feels responsible. At least give her a chance.'

'You think I should contact her?'

'I think it could be in your best interest. And I think you should drop all these stupid thoughts about getting back together with Steve.'

Beth gathered up their mugs and the cutlery and took them over to the sink. She squeezed some washing-up liquid into the bowl, washed the pots and left them drying on the drainer, all the while thinking about what Jan had said. She turned around to speak to her friend, but Jan was already halfway out of the door. 'Jan?'

'I'm off for a bath and an early night. I'm on the dreaded early shift tomorrow morning. I'll be back around lunch. Give me a call if you need anything.' Jan closed the door behind her.

Beth stood, staring into space. Contact Maureen? Should she?

# Chapter Four

Maureen's mobile rang. She pounced on her handbag and grabbed for the phone, her heart racing. She hesitated, trying to remember which button to press, then settled for the one on the left.

'Hello, Maureen. It's Beth. I saw your advert in the *West Briton*.'

Maureen's stomach turned somersaults as she clasped the phone with both hands. 'Oh, Beth, it's wonderful to hear from you. I've been so worried.' Her heart soared; thank God they weren't dead. 'How's Harrison?'

'He's good. I was wondering if you'd like to meet up for coffee?'

She breathed in deeply and tried to keep the excitement from her voice. 'Wonderful. How about tomorrow?' Did she sound too needy? She didn't want to scare Beth off.

'Could you come to Truro?'

'Name a time and place. I'll be there.'

'Do you know the café on the top floor of Waterstones?'

Maureen had fond memories of Waterstones. She'd spent many happy hours there with Anna, searching through the children's books, but she wasn't aware they had a café. 'I'll find it. Shall we say 10:00 a.m.?'

Maureen browsed through the bookshelves. Anna had always loved her books. At Harrison's age, Anna's favourite had been *The Very Hungry Caterpillar*. She would squeal with laughter when Maureen pretended to be a worm and wiggled her little finger through the holes in the various pictures of the food.

She picked up a copy but then realised that she had no idea what books Harrison already owned. She approached the lady behind the check-out desk, who looked up at her and smiled.

'I'm about to meet a young friend of mine in the café. If I buy him this book as a present, and it turns out he already has it, could I exchange it?'

'No need to pay for it now, Madam. Take it with you, and if it doesn't suit him, simply come back and choose something else.'

'I won't get arrested for shoplifting?'

'I think you'll find that half of those in the café reading books will be our "try before you buy" customers.'

Maureen thanked her and headed upstairs to the café. She glanced at her watch; it was still only a quarter to ten. Her eagerness to see Harrison had ensured she was on the platform at Falmouth Docks shortly after eight o'clock; at least fifteen minutes before the train was due in. She'd arrived in Truro at ten to nine. Even with a slow meander down from the station, it meant she'd still arrived at Waterstones three-quarters of an hour before she was supposed to meet them.

She ordered a small flat white and took a seat facing the entrance. To her right, sat an elderly gentleman leafing through what looked like a travel book on India. Maureen smiled to herself. Listen to her, she was in her mid-sixties and certainly did not think of herself as old, but he must be at least eighty, so she felt justified in thinking of him as such. She wondered if he was a fellow "try before you buy" customer. She opened the familiar pages of her book.

'Nana Mo, Nana Mo.' A small excited voice alerted Maureen to the arrival of Harrison and Beth.

Maureen stood, bent down to a child-friendly height and opened her arms as Harrison threw himself at her. She laughed and clutched at the table leg to steady her balance, then snuggled into his neck and breathed in the familiar smell of baby powder.

'Good morning, my little whirlwind. Would you like a milkshake?'

Harrison nodded his head up and down.

She looked up at Beth, who was hovering nervously. Surely this slip of a girl couldn't be violent? Steve must have been lying. 'And you, Beth. What can I get you?'

'My usual. Two shots, please.'

Maureen could never understand how Beth drank those small cups of sludgy espresso. The smell alone was enough to make her feel lightheaded. She decided on a second flat white for herself – a small one. She collected a tray and selected three chocolate chip cookies and a strawberry milkshake. She shuffled slowly along towards the till behind two young girls who seemed more interested in flirting with the young man behind the counter than ordering their coffee. She looked over to the table where Beth was removing Harrison's coat and strapping him into a booster seat.

Harrison squirmed, turned to look at her, and waved. 'Nana Mo!' he yelled.

Maureen blew him a kiss. He giggled and blew one back.

'Here we go.' Maureen put the tray on the table.

'Harry's?' Harrison picked up a cookie and looked at his mother.

'Nana Mo bought it for you. And the milkshake.' Beth put the bottle in front of him and inserted the straw. 'What do you say, Harrison?'

'Tank you.'

Maureen smiled. 'You're very welcome.' She put a beaker of crayons and a picture book on the table in front of him. 'Can you colour this for me?' She picked up a green crayon and began to shade in the grass. 'Like this.'

'Harry do it.'

He grabbed the crayon from her hand and began to scribble.

Beth stirred her coffee and glanced at the man on the next table. She lowered her voice. 'I'm pleased you agreed to see us. I feel awful about the last time we met. I was unbelievably rude.'

'Don't worry about it. Your life was in turmoil. It's understandable.'

'I'm really sorry,' Beth whispered. 'My friend, Jan, keeps tryin' to convince me I've nothin' to fear from Social Services. Unfortunately, I don't have her faith. I...' She looked over Maureen's shoulder to where two women were depositing their trays on the table next to them. 'Anyway, that's another story. When I realised you'd heard us arguin', and then when you mentioned the police and Social Services...well, I was terrified you'd report us. I'm afraid I ran.'

'I wouldn't do that Beth. I'd just like to help. I've become very fond of Harrison. Of you both that is. Have you found somewhere to stay?'

Beth shook her head, reached into her bag for a hanky, wiped the tears that were trickling down her cheeks and blew her nose.

'Jan's puttin' us up at her place, but it's not good. I'm sleepin' on the sofa and Harrison's on a blow-up mattress. Crap really.'

'What about your mum's?'

Beth snorted.

'I'm sorry, Beth. I'm not trying to stick my nose in where it's not wanted. I simply want to help you both.'

Tears trickled down Beth's cheeks. 'I'm sorry, can you watch him? I need the loo.' Beth disappeared in the direction of the ladies.

Harrison looked up from his colouring. 'Mummy?'

'She'll be back in a minute.' Maureen opened The *Very Hungry Caterpillar* book. 'Shall we look at this, Harrison? It's a lovely story.'

She shuffled her chair around beside him, moved the crayons and colouring book out of the way and began to read. *'In the light of the moon, a little egg lay on a leaf.'*

Harrison made loud slurping noises as the last of the milkshake bubbled up through the straw. He giggled.

Maureen continued to read, and wriggle her little finger through the holes in the fruit, pretending to be a worm. Harrison tried to catch her finger and giggled again. He was still giggling when Beth returned.

'Sorry I was so long. Have you been a good boy for Nana Mo?'

Harrison nodded.

'He's been perfect.' Maureen ruffled his hair and smiled at him.

The two women on the table behind them laughed loudly.

Maureen glanced over her shoulder before continuing. 'I was wondering if you might like to come over to my place for lunch tomorrow. Harrison could still have his afternoon nap, which would give us a chance to discuss your unfortunate situation in more conducive surroundings. I have an idea that I think might help. A possible solution. Shall we say around midday?'

Beth stroked her son's cheek then nodded. 'We'll come on the train. He'll enjoy that. You like trains, don't you, Harrison?'

Harrison grinned. 'Choo choo.'

Maureen put her empty coffee cup on the tray beside Beth's and added Harrison's empty bottle.

'Would you mind if I buy him this book? He hasn't got it already, has he?'

'He hasn't got any books, but he does like them. We sometimes get one from the library.'

Harrison nodded. 'I like storwies.'

'Well let's go and pay for this one, shall we?'

Harrison grinned.

They left the café and took the escalator down to the children's section where Maureen made the purchase. She handed the book in its paper bag over to Harrison who gripped it tightly to his chest as they walked out of the shop.

'I'll see you tomorrow then, about midday. It was lovely to see you both.'

Beth picked Harrison up. 'Say thank you to Nana Mo.'

'Tank you,' Harrison leaned forward in his mother's arms and landed a sloppy kiss on Maureen's cheek. 'See you tomylow.'

Maureen watched until they disappeared around the corner. She brushed away a tear. Their earlier coffee meetings in Falmouth had always been enjoyable, but this time it felt different. She hadn't been this happy since...since a very long time ago. Best not to think about those times now, not while she was in public.

Maureen pushed open the wooden gate, climbed the steps and opened the front door.

'Hello, I'm back,' she called up the stairs. 'Shall I put the kettle on?'

A deep voice boomed down the stairs. 'That would be good. Almost finished.'

Maureen shrugged off her coat and hung it in the cupboard under the stairs. She checked her appearance in the dark oak framed mirror that hung over the monk's settle, and patted a few stray grey hairs back into place. Slipping off her shoes, she opened the lid of the settle, dropped her shoes inside and reached for her slippers. They were new, black with embroidered flowers. She'd treated herself to them as a Christmas gift. She picked up her two shopping bags, carried them into the kitchen and switched on the kettle. Then she put the two bunches of flowers and salad items on the drainer, the milk, milkshake and pizza into the fridge and arranged the bananas and oranges in the fruit bowl.

She heard the heavy tread on the stairs and looked up as her neighbour and handyman, Bill entered the kitchen.

'I've finished making the bed, wardrobe and the bookcase, brought that box of books you wanted down from the loft and moved that cot downstairs into your spare room. I've just got the TV to unpack and set up now.'

'Thanks, Bill. I don't know where I'd be without you. The best part of living around here is having such wonderful neighbours.'

She left him drinking his coffee, climbed up to the third floor and entered the apartment. The small bedroom looked so much better with the junior bed in it. She pulled out the pillow, duvet cover and fitted sheet that she left overnight in the airing cupboard and carefully made up the bed. Next, she unpacked the box of Anna's books. Her head swirled with the memories that flooded back with each title. She sank onto the blue velvet beanbag and put the bigger books, one by one, in a row at the bottom: *The Wind in the Willows; The Secret Garden; The Faraway Tree;* and another favourite, *Peter Rabbit.* Anna would insist on a chapter from one every night before she would go to sleep. The picture books went on the middle shelf: *Where the Wild Things Are; The Snowman; Bambi.* These were the books they would read together on rainy days or on those numerous days when Anna was unwell. The top shelf was reserved for pocketbooks: *The Ugly Duckling; Dennis the Dragon; The Three Little Pigs.* These were a handy size for slipping into a handbag to read on a train or to take on a picnic.

'Oh, Anna, why couldn't our lives have been different? Why did we leave things until it was too late?'

'You okay, Maureen?' Bill asked as he walked in behind her.

'I'm fine. Just talking to myself.'

She looked around the room. It appeared just as she'd imagined after calling into Argos on the way home from Truro the previous afternoon. On impulse, she'd got off the train at the earlier stop and visited the store. The very kind sales assistant had promised the items would be delivered within four hours. She'd ordered the bed, wardrobe with a bottom drawer, blue velvet bean bag, bookcase and what was described as a 45in Smart TV with a Freeview tuner. She wasn't sure what that all meant, but he insisted it was the best and Maureen wanted everything to be perfect. The thought of losing Harrison from her life again sent cold shivers down her spine. Not another loss. He had to be part of her future. She couldn't face life without him.

# Chapter Five

Beth looked around the room in amazement. What was she doing here and why was Maureen showing her this? They'd finished the pizza lunch and then Maureen had said she wanted to show them something. Beth and Harrison had followed her up to the third floor of the house and into the hallway of what appeared to be a self-contained apartment. Maureen ushered them into the lounge.

A small beige leather sofa with cream crushed-velvet cushions and a comfortable looking chair with matching footstool looked inviting. Beth could imagine sitting here, watching the large wall-mounted TV and enjoying the simplicity of this room. A glass coffee table with soft plastic protectors on each corner, had been positioned in front of the sofa. It contained a cut-glass vase filled with a mixture of daffodils and narcissi. Their sweet perfume filled the room. She noticed that all the electrical sockets were protected with childproof covers. The walls and woodwork were painted white and two roof lights allowed sunlight to flood through the room.

She was lost for words as she followed Maureen through to the kitchen. A white table and chairs with bright red cushions stood in the centre. A cooker, dishwasher, fridge and washing machine, along with floor standing and wall cupboards, lined the walls. A large window above the sink and worktop revealed views through the treetops. This room had to be twice the size of the kitchen in her previous flat.

Still in a daze, Beth felt Harrison tug at her hand. 'Mummy, Mummy, look.' He pointed back into the lounge and ran towards a picnic hamper filled with soft toys, puzzles and wooden building bricks. 'My toys?'

'No, Harrison, they don't belong to you.'

'But you can play with them later.' Maureen took his hand. 'First let me show you the very best room, Harrison.' She led him back out through the hall and into the small bedroom.

Harrison gasped. 'Rocket. Moon. Stars!'

The walls were painted pale blue and decorated with transfers. The duvet cover and pillow continued the theme, with more images from space. He ran to the bed and stroked the bedclothes. Then he picked up the soft teddy bear from the pillow, hugged it, and gave it a big kiss. He sat down on the beanbag, took one of the picture books from the bookcase and began to leaf through the pages.

'Let me show you the rest of the flat, Beth. He seems happy enough for a minute.'

Beth followed Maureen into the central hallway.

'That door opens out onto a small balcony and a fire escape. The key lives on this hook above the door here, out of reach of little ones.' Maureen walked through another door, holding it open for Beth to enter. 'This is the main bedroom and the family bathroom is next door.'

Beth's head was spinning. Why had Maureen turned the top floor of her house into a two-bedroom apartment, all fitted out but, from what she could see, never used? And was she about to suggest that Beth and

Harrison could move in? More importantly, how did she feel about that possibility?

The place was amazing, but on the one hand, Maureen was nosy. Would they be able to live with her looking over their shoulders all the time? On the other hand, the flat was self-contained; she could always lock the door. This was much better than returning to the refuge. Or her mum's house. It was much more spacious and comfortable than Jan's place or even her old flat. Perhaps it could work.

'Shall we collect Harrison?' Maureen asked.

'Mm, not sure he'll want to go downstairs. He's probably too excited to settle down for his nap.'

Beth walked back into the small bedroom. Her heart flooded with love for her small son. He lay on the bed, sprawled on his back, one arm flung above his head while the other clutched the teddy to his chest. He was sound asleep.

Beth smiled at Maureen. 'He'll be off for at least an hour, I'm afraid. Dearovim. Will it be okay if I leave the bedroom door open and wait for him in the lounge?'

'I'll make us a cup of tea. We can just as easily talk things through up here. You go and sit down, make yourself at home.'

Home. Beth settled herself into the chair and put her feet up on the footstool. This place could be a wonderful home for the two of them. If she played her cards right, she could finish up paying less or even nothing at all for a far better home than their previous place next door.

Maureen arrived back and put the tea tray on the coffee table.

'How come you have your top floor all fitted out like this? Is it a holiday place for your family?'

Maureen frowned, poured Beth's tea and handed it to her. 'That's a long story. I'll tell you one day. But, for now, do you think that you and Harrison could be happy here?'

'It's awesome but too expensive for me. Sadly.'

'I don't need any rent. Look, I've just had to let my cleaning woman go. She was hopeless. Never dusted the skirting board at the back of the bed or polished the mirrors. How about you do a few hours of cleaning and my ironing for me each week, while I look after Harrison?'

Beth glanced around the room. This could be their new home, in exchange for a few hours of cleaning. She couldn't believe her good fortune. And free childcare thrown in.

Maureen finished her tea. 'I'll give you some time to think about it. There's tea, coffee, sugar and biscuits in the cupboard above the kettle and milk in the fridge. Help yourself. We'll talk about it when Harrison wakes up. I'll be downstairs.'

Beth listened to the door close behind Maureen. She tiptoed through to the small bedroom and checked on Harrison, who was snoring gently. How could she refuse? It was obvious that Harrison would love it here. Everything was perfect for him; his own room, a proper junior bed instead of a blow-up mattress, lots of toys and books. She would still be able to take him to the beach whenever he wanted. And to the local playgroup twice a week to play with his little friends – especially Percy and Bea, who he loved.

She lay back in the chair and listened to the woodpigeons call to each other as they perched in the trees outside. Comfortable, she dozed off, only waking when she heard Harrison shout out for her. She ran to the bedroom door. He was sitting up in bed, still clutching the teddy, and smiling.

'Harry's bed,' he giggled. 'Harry's bear.'

'Do you like it here, Harrison?'

'Harry's home?'

'Shall we go and tell Maureen that we'd like to stay?'

Harrison jumped out of bed, grabbed her hand and dragged her to the door. 'Nana Mo!' he yelled.

Maureen stood at the bottom of the stairs, smiling up at them. She reminded Beth of the cat in *Alice in Wonderland*. She had a satisfied, possibly even smug, smile on her face.

# Chapter Six

Maureen reached for the hot chocolate and leaned back on her pillow. The time had simply flown by since Beth and Harrison had moved in three months before. Her mornings were filled with joy as she looked after Harrison, doing puzzles, flashcards, watching CBeebies or Netflix while Beth dusted, vacuumed and cleaned. Maureen was pleasantly surprised to find how seriously Beth took her cleaning responsibilities, and also, how thorough she was. The tiles in Maureen's bathrooms had never sparkled as they did now under Beth's care.

After lunch, Beth would then take Maureen's laundry off the washing line and take it up to the apartment to iron while Harrison had his nap. Although she'd always paid for a cleaner, Maureen had never employed anyone to do her ironing before. She always hated ironing with a passion and now used this free time to catch up on her reading. Beth had freed Maureen from all the boring tasks in her life and replaced them instead with the enjoyment of sharing Harrison.

She drained her cup and put it on the bedside cabinet. Drowsiness drifted over her. Half asleep, she became vaguely aware of voices above her. Beth's voice and, unless she was mistaken, a man's. Surely, she'd made it clear enough; the one thing she would not tolerate was Beth entertaining male visitors.

She got up, put on her dressing gown, tiptoed to the window and listened again. The voices were low but undeniable. She clenched her fists as the anger surged through her. How dare Beth break the only rule of the house? Beth getting mixed up with some man was the last thing Maureen wanted. What would happen if she decided to move in with him and take Harrison with her? The desolation in her day-to-day existence had been swept aside by the arrival of Harrison. She couldn't go back to a life without him. It didn't bear thinking about.

She wanted to storm upstairs and confront Beth, but that was bound to create a difficult situation and probably wake Harrison, who would presumably find it rather frightening to find a strange man in his home.

As she reached over to flick on the bedroom light, she heard the distinctive noise of the balcony door closing above her. Heavy footsteps clattered down the fire escape. Ignoring the light, she turned back to the window, pushed up the blind and saw the unmistakable outline of a man as he jumped from the bottom step. A large man, with enormous shoulders. She recognised that physique.

Steve.


Maureen woke early the next morning. Unable to go back to sleep, she'd opened the bedroom blind and gazed out over her pristine back garden. Of course, these days she employed a gardener one morning a week. He would cut the grass and do any of the heavier work, like digging over the vegetable patch and pruning her fruit trees. But she enjoyed planting the borders and just generally pottering.

The early morning sun had already burnt through the mist and the temperature was pleasantly mild for the first week in May. She could smell the sea and hear the crashing of the waves. She did so love being this close to the beach. Harrison also loved it. The two of them would often meander down to Castle Beach while Beth was cleaning. Harrison's favourite game was to pick up small stones and hurl them into the rock pools. He also loved to collect sea glass fragments, smoothed and rounded by the action of the sea. They would bring them home and add them to their collection in the glass bowl on Maureen's kitchen windowsill, where they sparkled like tiny jewels in the sunlight.

She decided to enjoy her breakfast on the patio. As she carried her tray of tea and toast outside, her tame male blackbird launched into his rich mating song, varied and flute-like. She glanced over to his usual perch on the apple tree. This was the bird's third season in Maureen's garden. He was easy to identify because he was partially albino with white tail feathers and patches on his back. She noticed that the apple tree was just coming into bud, two weeks earlier than the previous year. Usually, this combination of pleasures would uplift her spirits. This morning they failed to do so.

Sat at her patio table, she sipped her tea, spread her toast with marmalade and pondered over what she was going to say to Beth. How should she approach this? It was a delicate subject, a difficult balance. She didn't want to upset Beth to the point that she felt uncomfortable and left, but she couldn't ignore the fact that, by inviting Steve to her room, Beth had deceived her. Why was it that everyone eventually betrayed her?

She could hear Beth and Harrison talking in their kitchen above her, and she made her decision. She would confront Beth in a way that would make her recognise Maureen's suspicions but allowed her a way out. She glanced at her watch: seven-thirty. Not too early for a visit, especially if she pretended it was to plan a treat. It promised to be such a lovely day, just the kind to suggest that they should go on a picnic.

She climbed the two flights of stairs and knocked on the door of the apartment.

Beth called out, 'Come in. We're in the kitchen havin' breakfast.'

'Morning, Nana Mo,' Harrison said.

Maureen kissed the top of his head and sat beside him.

'Cup of tea? Or a slice of toast?' Beth asked.

'I've just had my breakfast in the garden. In fact, that's why I'm here. I heard you chatting and realised you were up and about. I wondered, as it's such a lovely day, if we might take a picnic and go to the beach.' She turned to Harrison. 'What do you think, Harrison? Would you like to go to the beach and have a paddle? You like picnics, don't you?'

Harrison nodded. 'Ham, cheese, cwackers.'

'I'm sure we can arrange that.' Maureen put her hand over her mouth and yawned. 'Excuse me. I didn't sleep very well last night. I kept hearing your TV, which is unusual.'

Beth began to load the dishwasher. Maureen saw the blush as it rose from Beth's neckline and spread across her cheek.

'I'm so sorry, Maureen. I fell asleep in the chair. When I woke up there was one of those late-night chat shows on. It won't happen again.'

Maureen stood, kissed Harrison on his cheek and moved to the kitchen door. 'I'll see myself out, Beth. Don't worry, I'll make the picnic. Shall we aim to leave at about ten o'clock?'

'We'll come down and find you. Say goodbye, Harrison.'

'Bye-bye.'

Maureen walked into the hall and then turned to look at the balcony door.

The key was in the lock.

Beth followed Maureen into the hall. She saw Maureen turn towards the balcony door and then glance back at her, before walking out of the front door and down the stairs. Beth wondered what that last look from Maureen had been about. It reminded her of her mother and those "Oh Beth" moments.

'I've failed all my GCSE's, but don't worry...I've got a job washin' glasses at Weatherspoons.'

'Oh, Beth.'

She had no idea of where her mum's sense of superiority came from. She might boast of running her own business, but she was only a cleaner. Washing glasses was no worse than cleaning up other people's muck.

'I'm pregnant, but don't worry...Ron's agreed to marry me.'

'Oh, Beth.'

Ron *had* married her. Beth's own father had disappeared, never to be seen again, as soon as her mum told him she was pregnant.

'I've split up with Steve and lost the flat, but don't worry…I've been offered a much better self-contained apartment next door.'

'Oh, Beth.'

Her mother's home was a crappy flat on an estate that was once owned by the council but now belonged to a private landlord. He refused to spend money on repairs; it would reduce his profit margin. As a result, the flat suffered from mouldy walls, cracked glass in the windows and a faulty boiler that only worked every other Sunday – and then, only if there *wasn't* an R in the month.

At least Maureen had stopped short of saying "Oh, Beth," but that look worried her.

She looked over to the balcony door. Shit, she'd left the key in the lock. How could she have made such a stupid mistake? She blamed her hormones. Her thoughts had been so full of Steve and their steamy night of passion. How she'd missed that over the past three months. Jan had told her to stay away from Steve, and Maureen had been very clear about the ban on male visitors, but the illicit nature of their meeting had only made it more exciting.

She'd rung Steve the previous morning, while Harrison was still asleep. He'd been only too pleased to let bygones be bygones, and was eager to visit her that evening. She'd told him to come in off Melville Road, through the back gate and up the fire escape.

One thing was for sure; she wouldn't be able to smuggle Steve in again. She'd have to find another way to see him in future.

# Chapter Seven

Maureen sat in her lounge, drinking an afternoon cup of tea, engrossed in the book she was reading. There was a gentle tap on her door. It burst open and Harrison raced across to her chair and threw himself at her knees, hugging them tightly. She leaned over and kissed the top of his head.

'Good afternoon, sweetie. Are you going out?'

'We're nippin' to Event Square to fetch some milk.' Beth stood at the door. 'You want owt?'

'I'm good, thank you. But isn't your mother due?'

'She said she'd get in on the two-twenty train, so we've plenty of time. See you in half an hour. Say goodbye, Harrison.'

'Bye-bye, Nana Mo.'

'Bye-bye, my little cupcake.'

Five minutes later, the doorbell rang. Maureen opened the front door. A small woman, both short in stature and slight of frame, stood on the doorstep.

'You must be Mrs Rowe. I'm Maureen James. We spoke on the phone a few months ago.'

'How do.'

Maureen remembered from the telephone call how thick Mrs Rowe's Cornish accent was. She'd had trouble then understanding her. She opened the door wide. 'Come in. You're a bit early. I'll make you a cup of tea.

Beth and Harrison will be back shortly. They've just gone to the shop.'

Mrs Rowe stepped into the hall and looked around. 'Trains into Bodmin were running late. Problems up country at Dawlish, as usual. I caught the earlier train late if you catch my meaning.'

Maureen led Mrs Rowe through to the kitchen.

'My Gar!' Mrs Rowe walked over to the sink and gazed out of the window. 'Fine-looking garden. Beth's place next door were covered in tarmac – nowhere for kids to play. Told you Beth always comes up smelling of roses.'

'It's a pleasure having them stay here. Harrison's an absolute dear.'

'I'm sure. But 'e's an 'andful, especially at our age. Too much for me.'

Maureen smiled with relief. She'd been worried that Mrs Rowe might be here to persuade Beth to move back with her. She put the teapot on her silver tray, with matching milk jug and sugar bowl. 'Milk?'

Mrs Rowe nodded. 'Ta, I'm chacking.'

Maureen handed Mrs Rowe a cup of tea.

'So, Beth behaving 'erself?'

'In what way?'

'Stayed off the booze?'

There it was again, that undertone of condemnation. 'You really don't have a very high opinion of your daughter, do you?'

Mrs Rowe ladled three spoons of sugar into her cup. 'Nor would you if you'd seen 'ow she treated Ron. A saint that man, and bleddy rich.' She picked up the spoon and stirred vigorously.

'Rich? I thought he was in the navy?'

'What? Oh, you mean bleddy rich? It means nice guy, 'ansome, 'e were lovely.'

'But I understood he was violent towards her.'

Mrs Rowe laughed. 'Giss on! Beth were the violent one. Can't hold a drink. Makes 'er vicious. Came to see me before 'e went back to sea, covered in bruises.' She sipped her tea. Ron put in for custody, but Social Services eventually decided the boy'd be better with Beth. They gave 'er a tough time though. Touch and go for a while.'

'I think she's an excellent mother.' Maureen picked up her empty cup, turned her back on Mrs Rowe and emptied the dregs into the sink. 'That sounds like her now. We're in here, Beth.'

'Hello, Mum. You're early.'

'Me and Maureen 'ave been getting to know each other. How do, Harrison. My Gar you've grown.'

Harrison clung to his mother's legs and sucked his thumb.

'Well he will have, won't he? You haven't seen him for twelve months.'

'If you're going to show me this flat, we'd best get a wiggle on.' Mrs Rowe walked towards her daughter but made no attempt to hug her or offer a peck on the cheek. 'I'm catching the twenty after four to Truro. It's my Bingo night. Right on then, Maureen. Nice to meet you.'

The office didn't smell any different than it had on Maureen's first visit. A musty, almost damp smell pervaded the room, which probably stemmed from the row upon row of old legal books that lined the walls. Alternatively, the odour could be coming from the piles of brown folders, tied with pink ribbons, draped over every available surface, including the floor.

Maureen and Giles had visited this firm of solicitors over thirty-five years before, to sign their wills, along with all the contract papers on their Emilia Boulevard house purchase. Of course, it had been the appropriately named Mr Wills Senior who looked after them then. Today she sat opposite his son, Mr Wills Junior. Apparently, his father, now a widower, had retired ten years before and bought himself a motorbike and a few acres of woodland.

'I see very little of him these days. He's either coppicing trees or taking long rides through unlikely foreign countries. Uzbekistan was his last foray.'

'Gosh! I don't even own a passport. Scotland's the furthest I've ever been – and that was for our honeymoon.' Maureen had always toyed with the idea of visiting the Galapagos Islands but, even though the tours were described as *fully escorted,* they always seemed a little too adventurous for her liking.

'What can I do for you today, Mrs James?'

'I want to change my will. I thought it was for the best – bring it up to date.'

'Quite.'

'I've drafted out the details but it needs putting into legalese.' Maureen handed over the paper she'd extracted from her handbag.'

Mr Wills glanced at them. His right eyebrow arched. 'And how old is this Harrison Taylor?'

'He'll be three in June.'

'Not a toy boy then?'

Maureen laughed. 'He's a boy who likes toys, and he's the love of my life, but not in the way you mean.'

Mr Wills Junior continued to read through her notes. 'This all seems straightforward. I could have it drawn up and ready for you to sign next week if that's alright?'

Maureen nodded. 'I also want you to draw up the necessary papers for me to be named as his legal guardian in the event of his mother being unable to look after him.'

'Is that likely?'

'I want them both to have the security. You see they are living with me at the moment. His grandmother isn't interested in either of them. Harrison's father is…well he died shortly after Harrison was born. He was killed whilst on active service. If anything happened to Beth, I would want to be able to give Harrison a home rather than him going into foster care or, God forbid, a Children's Home.'

'I can draw up the papers for you, but his mother would have to sign her agreement.'

'I can understand that. There shouldn't be a problem.'

Maureen stood, shook the solicitor's hand and agreed to return the following Thursday at ten o'clock.

# Chapter Eight

Maureen opened the bottle of red wine she'd collected earlier from the local wine merchant. The owner had assured her that this particular brand was a medal winner, with an exceptional bouquet. It needed to be at the price he charged. Giles always said that good red wine needed time to breathe. He would not be impressed with her efforts and would say it should have been opened much earlier. He always took care to make sure their wine was the correct temperature, allowed sufficient time to breathe and poured slowly to avoid sediment. They always treated themselves to a bottle on a Friday night. One large glass each with their pasta, and the second glass as they sat in the lounge after the meal.

She glanced at her watch: seven-thirty. She'd told Beth there was something they needed to discuss before she went out. Beth had agreed to come down and bring the baby monitor as soon as Harrison went off to sleep.

Maureen put two cut crystal wine glasses onto her silver tray, added the bottle of wine and carried them into the lounge, where she placed them on the coffee table. She opened the bureau, took out the large manila envelope she'd collected from her solicitor the day before, and put it beside the drinks tray. She went into the kitchen, opened the cutlery draw and selected one of her steak knives. She returned to the lounge and put the knife next to the envelope.

Beth walked in behind her. 'What's up, Maureen? Expecting company?'

Maureen turned around. Beth was wearing tight jeans and suede boots, with a long-sleeved cream blouse. Unusually, she was wearing makeup, which was immaculate: pale pink lipstick, dark brown eye shadow and lashings of mascara.

'You look lovely, Beth.'

'Thanks. What do you want to talk to me about? It sounded serious.'

Maureen waved at the chair. 'Sit down. I won't keep you long. What time are you meeting Jan?'

Beth glanced at her watch. 'I'm okay for an hour. Need to leave just before half-eight so I can walk into town to meet her.'

Maureen knew very well that Beth was meeting Steve at eight-thirty, at the bottom of Melville road, because she'd overheard Beth organising it. Maureen had been sitting on the patio enjoying her breakfast when Beth called Steve to make the arrangements. It was another pleasant day, sunny and mild, and Beth's kitchen window had been wide open.

'I wanted you to know that I've changed my will.' Maureen nodded at the envelope on the tray. 'Apart from a few donations to charities, the whole of my estate will go to Harrison when I die.'

Beth gasped. 'Why would you do that? I thought you had a daughter.'

'I did. Anna would be twenty-seven this year. But she died seven years ago.'

'Bloody Hell, Maureen! I'm so sorry.'

Maureen walked over to the bureau and took out a couple of small photographs. She handed one to Beth.

'This was Anna and Giles at Kayak cove, our favourite picnic spot. Anna was about one there, just started walking.' She brushed aside a tear. 'And this was her at nineteen.' She passed the second picture to Beth. 'I was expecting her to start at Exeter University the following year, but unfortunately, she met Tony and decided, after only three weeks, that she wanted to marry him. I made her promise to wait until after she'd finished university, hoping she'd come to her senses while she was away. Instead, she eloped.'

'Oh, Maureen, you poor thing.'

'I was so hurt by her betrayal that I refused to answer her calls or see her for nearly a year, until she came to see me a month before their baby was due. Tony had been knocking her about. I begged her to leave him. She agreed, but it was too late.'

'What happened?'

'She was killed by her husband…Tony…my son-in-law. I went to collect her, but I got to her too late…so my grandson also died.'

Maureen watched as Beth paled beneath her make-up. 'Why would he do that?'

'I'd persuaded Anna to come and live with me, which is why I had the third floor fitted out as an apartment. Her relationship with Tony had deteriorated and became very abusive. Unfortunately, when she told him she was leaving, he attacked her. She'd been an asthmatic since birth. He knocked her about so badly that it brought on a severe attack.'

Maureen reached for a tissue from her cardigan pocket. She blew her nose, wiped away a tear and looked into Beth's eyes. 'She died, and the baby died with her. I was left with nothing. Anna was only five when Giles died. I brought her up on my own, so we were extremely close, until…After she died, I felt a huge sense of guilt about our estrangement. Perhaps, if I hadn't turned my back on her for a year, it would have all ended differently. I realised too late that she was my reason for living… Anna and her unborn son were my future.'

Beth moved from the sofa, knelt in front of Maureen's chair and held her hands. 'I can't imagine owt worse. Poor you. No wonder my arguin' with Steve upset you so much. Was Tony charged with manslaughter?'

'I found him in the kitchen, flat on his face in a pool of blood. Stabbed through the heart. Quite literally fell on his sword. Or rather, his carving knife.'

Beth stood, put her arms across Maureen's shoulder and sat on the chair arm. 'How did you get through somethin' so awful?'

'My life became a day to day existence. There was no joy, nothing to look forward to…That is until I met you and Harrison.' Maureen smiled at Beth. 'Have a glass of wine with me, Beth.'

'I'd love one, Maureen, but I really shouldn't drink.'

'Please, I don't like to drink alone, and I really do feel like I need one. Just a small one while you look through these papers?' Maureen picked up the bottle, poured wine into two glasses and handed one to Beth.

'Thanks, Maureen.' Beth took a sip of wine and smiled. 'Crickey, Maureen, that's a drop of the good stuff.'

Maureen reached for the envelope, picked up the knife and sliced it open. She pulled out two sets of papers.

'This one is my will.' She put it on the coffee table. 'And this one is a legal agreement. I know how worried you have been in the past, about Social Services and your fear of Harrison being taken into care. This document means that if anything happens that prevents you from looking after Harrison for a while, for example, if you were ill or involved in an accident, then I would become his legal guardian and he could stay living here until you recovered. It would mean Social Services wouldn't be able to argue that I wasn't a relative or had any right to help and they wouldn't be able to put him into foster care or a home. I know it's unlikely, but I thought it would give us all peace of mind.'

'I don't know what to say, Maureen. You're so thoughtful.'

'Cheers,' Maureen raised her glass and clinked it against Beth's.

Beth sat back on the sofa and glanced through the papers while she sipped her wine. After about fifteen minutes, Beth put both her empty glass and the papers onto the coffee table.

'Got a pen?'

Maureen handed her the ballpoint she kept in the side pocket of her chair. She watched as Beth signed the papers and then topped up her glass.

'I hope we never need those,' Maureen pointed at the signed guardianship papers, 'and I hope it's some time before Harrison comes into his inheritance. I enjoy my life so much these days, I wouldn't like to think of it coming to an end just yet. Harrison has rekindled feelings of joy and happiness I haven't experienced for many years. Cheers.' She raised her glass to Beth. 'Here's to Harrison, who deserves the best possible start in life.'

'That's all I've ever wanted for him.' Beth chinked her glass against Maureen's.

Maureen sipped her wine and murmured. 'And that's what he will have.'

# Chapter Nine

Beth opened her eyes and then closed them again quickly. Her head pounded. She tried again. Her white bedroom walls were now pale blue, the Laura Ashley bedclothes had been replaced with dark blue brushed cotton and her brass headboard was non-existent. Where the hell was she? And why was she lying in a strange bed, fully clothed?

The last thing she remembered was arguing with Steve after he'd arrived in Falmouth, ten minutes late. They must have come back to his place. Shame she couldn't remember the rest of the evening; she'd been looking forward to a night of fun and frolics. She glanced at the bedside clock: 5:00 a.m. Shit! Maureen would have kittens. Perhaps she could get Steve to drive her home now, before Maureen woke and realised that she'd been out all night. But where was he?

'Steve!' she yelled.

No answer. Perhaps he was in the bathroom, wherever that was.

She lifted her head from the pillow. The room spun around and tilted. Yuk, she swallowed back the salty bile. Pushing aside the covers, she swung her legs out of bed and levered herself up on her elbows until, with a huge sense of achievement, she eventually managed to sit on the edge with her feet on the floor. Standing was more precarious, but after a short while, her head cleared a little and she took a tentative step towards the bedroom door. So far so good.

The door opened onto what appeared to be a narrow hallway. She felt for the light switch and flicked it on. The hall had a Victorian tiled floor and the walls were painted with rich burgundy paint. She couldn't remember this at all. Where was she?

'Steve?'

Nothing.

The door opposite was open, revealing a sofa covered in bright orange throws, a small plastic side table and a wall-mounted TV. She guessed the room immediately to her right was the bathroom, ignored it, and walked to the door at the end of the hall. She peeped into the room. A kitchen. Good, she could kill for a glass of cold water. She pushed back the door, stepped into the room, and gasped. Steve lay crumpled on the floor, his back towards her. She bent down and reached for his shoulder.

'Come on, you stupid bugger. It's not like you to keel over after too much drink.'

She pulled him towards her so that he rolled onto his back. For a second, she wondered why he was wearing what looked like a red map of Australia across his yellow T-shirt until, suddenly, with gut-wrenching realisation, she recognised it as a stain of congealing blood. At the side of his body, also covered in blood, was a knife. She screamed. Her legs gave way and she collapsed onto her knees beside him.

'Steve, wake up, wake up.' She reached for his hand. Cold. She tried feeling for a pulse in his neck, his wrist. Nothing.

Her handbag sat on the kitchen table. She couldn't remember how it got there, but then, she couldn't remember any of last night. She stood, clutched the worktop while she waited for the dizziness to stop, then tip-toed around Steve's body and grabbed her phone from her bag. She pressed contacts and clicked on Jan's number.

'Hi, Beth. What gets you up so early?' Jan sounded worried 'Is Harrison okay?'

'Steve's dead. He's been murdered. Please come and fetch me.'

'What!'

'I'm at his place in Helston. He's here, on his kitchen floor. No pulse, he's cold, blood everywhere. He's definitely dead.'

'Have you called the police?'

'Please come and fetch me. I need to get back to Harrison before he wakes up.'

'Beth, I'm at Heathrow picking up a client. I won't be back 'til lunch-time. Look, I'll help you in any way I can, but you can't run away from this. You *have* to call the police. Do you understand?'

'Jan?'

'Sorry, Beth, I'm going to hang up now so that you can ring them. Ring 999. Now, Beth!'

The phone went dead.

Beth sank back to the floor and rested her back on the kitchen units. This was a nightmare. How had it happened? Why had it happened? Who would want to kill Steve? She rubbed her forehead. This headache was making it impossible for her to think clearly. If she rang 999 she'd probably be a suspect – especially as she couldn't remember a thing. But, then again, if she crept away, the police could find evidence that she'd been here, which would make her look guilty.

She breathed deeply and tried to calm her racing pulse. Of course, Jan was right. Jan was always right, always the sensible one. She needed to ring the police. She sighed, lifted her mobile, tapped in 999 and pressed call.

Maureen woke with a start. She glanced at the monitor at the side of the bed. No sound from Harrison, so what had woken her? The front doorbell rang, followed by a heavy banging. She threw on her dressing gown, stuffed the monitor into her pocket and pushed her feet into her slippers.

'I'm coming, I'm coming!' She hurried down the stairs.

Two uniformed police officers stood on the doorstep. Maureen's pulse pounded in her ears.

'Good morning,' the male officer said. 'I'm Sergeant Dale and this…' He pointed to his female colleague…'is Police Constable Thompson.' They both held up their warrant cards. 'May we come in?'

'Whatever's the matter? Has someone been hurt?' Maureen opened the door wide and ushered them into the lounge.

'I take it you're Mrs Maureen James?'

'What's this all about, officer?'

'Please, madam. Take a seat.'

She sank into the chair, her heart and thoughts racing.

The two officers perched on the sofa. Sergeant Dale took out his notebook and smiled at Maureen. 'Could you confirm that Mrs Beth Taylor lives with you?'

'She and her son, Harrison, are in the top floor apartment. Shall I fetch her?'

'She's not there, Mrs James.'

'What do you mean? Of course she is.'

'We're investigating a suspicious death, and–'

'Not Beth. Please don't tell me Beth's dead?'

'We're investigating the suspicious death of a Mr Steve Allen.'

'Steve?'

'Do you know the gentleman?'

'Who would want to kill Steve?'

'Mummy.' Harrison's small voice could be heard over the monitor.

Maureen leapt to her feet. 'I'm sorry, that's Harrison. I'll have to go to him.'

Sergeant Dale nodded. Maureen raced up the two flights of stairs and into the hall of the apartment. Beth had left the door unlocked so Maureen could check on Harrison. She ran into his room. He sat on his bed, clutching his rabbit and teddy bear.

'Mummy?'

'She'll be back soon, darling. Shall we go downstairs?'

Harrison nodded.

Maureen held his hand as they walked down the stairs. 'The police have come to see us. Isn't that exciting?'

He nodded again. 'Car?'

'That's right. You've got one, haven't you?'

'Harry's car.' He raced into the lounge, ran to his toy box, pulled out his police car and rushed over to the coffee table. 'Brum, Brum, nee nah, nee nah.' He pushed his toy along the tabletop, and glanced up at the two police officers with a shy smile.

PC Thompson smiled back at him. 'That's a lovely car. Would you like to sit in a real police car, Harrison?'

Harrison nodded. She took his hand and steered him towards the door.

'Stop! Where are you taking him?'

'He'll be fine with me, Mrs James. Its better he doesn't hear what my colleague has to say. We'll be back shortly.'

Maureen watched Harrison grab the police woman's outstretched hand. How dare she take him away from her? He needed her.

Sergeant Dale returned to his notebook. 'How well did you know Steve Allen?'

'I only met him once.' Maureen leaned forward in her chair. 'Where's Beth? Has she been hurt?'

'She's fine. She's helping us with our enquiries.'

Sergeant Dale asked about Beth's next of kin, wrote down her mother's details, and asked if she knew the name of Beth's ex-husband's ship. He made a few more entries in his notebook, snapped it shut and looked up at Maureen. 'Okay, we're done here, I'll catch up with my colleague and you can rescue Harrison.' He smiled at her. 'He's a bonny lad, 'ansome.'

Maureen's heart swelled with pride. 'He's adorable.' She walked with him to the door. 'So, what's happening with Beth? Will she be back later?'

'Unlikely. Are you okay looking after Harrison for now? I imagine Social Services will be in touch later this morning.'

'We'll be fine. We don't need Social Services. I'm his legal guardian.'

'That's good, but they will still have to visit. They always do in these circumstances.'

'These circumstances?'

'Try not to worry.'

Maureen followed him down the steps. She hoped no one saw her, dressed in her slippers and dressing gown, being accompanied by a policeman. What on earth would they think?

Harrison sat in the passenger seat wearing PC Thompson's hat. He shouted through the open window. 'Look, Nana Mo.' He reached over to the dashboard and pressed a button, then pointed up to the car roof, where the blue lights flickered.

'I'm glad he hasn't found the siren,' Maureen said. 'Come on. Let's be having you, young man.' She opened the car door and helped him clamber out.

'We'll be in touch as soon as we have any news, either later today, or early tomorrow.' Sergeant Dale got into the car and waved to Harrison as they pulled away.

Maureen steered Harrison through the gate and up the steps.

'Time for breakfast, Harrison,' she said, her voice perfectly cheerful.

Maureen sipped her coffee. The monitor sat on the table in front of her. Harrison had asked to go down for his midday nap at eleven. It must have been the excitement of the police car and the visit from Social Services. The case officer had asked Maureen, and Harrison lots of questions, checked the signed legal papers carefully and confirmed that he was happy with the guardianship arrangements. But he warned her, it would have to be approved by the family court. He must have noticed her frown and assured her that he, as a representative of Social Services, would recommend that Harrison remained in Maureen's care.

Now she was alone and grateful for the chance to think. Her thoughts were still full of the latest news from Sergeant Dale. He'd telephoned to tell her that Beth had been charged with Steve's murder and remanded in custody. Maureen had enquired about bail but was told it was unlikely.

Maureen thought back over the previous evening. Had she done the right thing? Of course, she knew that Beth had lied to her and was meeting Steve. She also knew that something had to be done to split Beth and Steve up before there was any chance of them moving in together and taking Harrison with them. She knew that even if she managed that, Beth was a young woman, and likely to meet someone else in time, putting her relationship with Harrison in jeopardy again and again. And she knew that Beth got argumentative, even violent when she drank. Had she gone too far?

But the truth was, with Beth arrested for murder, the future now looked very different. This would be described by Giles as "the other side of the coin." She could think this through from the opposite perspective.

She glanced at the monitor. Silence, bless him.

One thing she knew for sure, Harrison had to remain her priority. No one would be able to prove that she'd known Beth was seeing Steve last night. If she now said nothing and allowed things to take their toll, she would remain Harrison's guardian. Even better, if Beth was found guilty and sent to prison, Maureen would get to enjoy the pleasure of a future with Harrison all to herself.

She leaned back in her chair and sighed.

# Chapter Ten

The door opened.

'Oh, there you are, Jane. Miss Taylor is processed and ready to be shown to her cell now.'

'It's Mrs Taylor,' Beth said.

'Oh, I'm *sorry*.' The prison officer sneered at Beth. '*Mrs* Taylor is ready to be shown to her cell now.'

Beth flinched.

'This way' the warder said. 'Don't forget your stuff.'

Beth picked up the small cardboard box containing her belongings – or at least those she'd been allowed to keep with her – and followed the warder out through a different door from the one she'd arrived by. It led into a corridor.

As the warder locked the door behind them, she glanced across at Beth. 'Don't mind her. She's like that with everyone. Don't take it personally.'

Beth shrugged. 'I'll try.'

'I'm Jane, as you probably gathered from Godzilla. Do you want to be called Mrs Taylor or would you prefer us to call you by your first name?'

'It's Beth. I guess Mrs Taylor's a bit...you know... stuffy.'

They walked down a white-painted corridor on a blue swirly-patterned carpet. White wooden doors, each labelled with a brass nameplate, were spaced evenly along either side. Offices, Beth presumed. They reached a solid-looking wooden door with a small glass viewing panel. A young woman in a warder's uniform sat beside it on a chair. She struggled to her feet as they approached. Beth noticed she was heavily pregnant.

'Hi, Jane,' she said. 'You still on duty?'

'Volunteered for a double shift. Need the dosh for my holiday. How long have you got now?'

'Due date's 14$^{th}$ June. I'll probably go off at the end of the month – at the May bank holiday. I was going to work up to the first twinges, but I'm not keen on these light duties. Booorring.'

'I know what you mean, but the last thing you need is a thump on the bump.'

'That's what the Guv' said, but it seems like a long shift, sat here all day.'

The young woman unlocked the door for them and then stood back, flattening herself against the wall, so that Beth and Jane could pass by her and into yet another corridor. The door closed behind them. Beth heard the lock turn as Jane led her down the new corridor, their footsteps echoing on the tiled floor. Beth's nose tickled with the smell of bleach. They turned a corner and came to another locked door. This one was metal with a glass viewing panel strengthened with wire mesh. Jane pressed a buzzer. A face appeared at the window, followed by the clunk of a key turning in the lock.

Beth's heart sank as the door opened. A big, tall, unfriendly-looking woman stood beside the door, her tunic buttons strained across her bosom. Beth estimated that her uniform had to be at least two sizes too small. A wet patch could be seen under her raised arm as she held the door open. The stench of BO wafted over Beth.

'Welcome to the Hotel California – otherwise known as A Block.' The woman laughed harshly but didn't crack a smile as they crossed the threshold.

Beth looked around. In front of her was a typical scene that she'd seen countless times on TV shows. A metal staircase led from halfway down the large hall type space, up to the first floor. Cell doors were distributed evenly along each side of the wall, upstairs and down. Large nets hung across from one balcony to the other, presumably to stop anyone from jumping – or at least from doing themselves much damage if they did.

'You're down here.' Jane led Beth to a door on the ground floor, close to the staircase. She unlocked it and ushered Beth in. 'This will be your home base between 7:00 p.m. and 7:30 a.m. every day, for the next few months, I guess. 'Til your court case.'

Beth walked around the small space. It was better than she'd expected. A cubicle in the corner of the room housed a toilet, hand-basin and shower. It didn't have a door, but at least it gave some privacy.

Jane picked up a plastic bag and towel from the single bed. 'You can buy toiletries from the prison shop in the morning, but they're closed right now. These should get you through 'til then.'

'Thanks.' Beth took the towel and bag and inspected the contents. It contained a toothbrush, mini toothpaste, comb and a small bar of soap. The sort of thing you'd find in a hotel room.

'Here's your supper.' Jane picked up a small, brown paper carrier bag from the bedside table and handed it to Beth.

Beth peeped inside and saw a packet of cheese sandwiches, a bag of crisps and a bottle of water. 'Do I get to meet any of the others, or am I to be all by myself?'

'You room alone, but mealtimes are usually taken together in the canteen. This supper snack is a one-off, so you can settle in. Breakfast begins at 7:30, tea or coffee, toast and either porridge or cereal – except on Sundays when you get eggs. Then you'll be collected from the canteen and inducted into your new role – cleaning toilets.'

'You're jokin' me!'

'I'm sorry, but your admission form states that your only work experience 'til now, is bar work and cleaning. As you can imagine, we don't have much call for barmaids here.'

So, this was what her life had come to, cleaning up other people's crap. 'Please, there must be somethin' else I could do?'

'Someone has to do it. But don't worry…it's only 'til it's allocated to another newbie in a couple of weeks. Then you'll move onto something else. Lunch is next, served back in the canteen – a choice of sandwiches and a mug of tea, followed by floor cleaning duties in the afternoon.'

'What about fresh air and exercise.'

'Well, we can't arrange any trips to the park, but you'll be allowed an hour in the courtyard after dinner. It's not very big, but you could always walk round and round in circles. If you don't fancy that, there's the TV lounge, the gym, pool or ping pong.'

'Pool? Great, I love swimmin'.'

Jane laughed. 'Pool, as in billiards.'

Beth bit her lip and tried, but failed, to stop the tears from trickling down her cheeks.

'Come on Beth...it's not too bad here. I've worked in far worse places.'

Beth sank onto the bed and buried her head in her hands.

'Okay, I'll leave you to it. Someone will be here at 7:30 a.m. to take you to the canteen. Goodnight.' Jane left, slamming the metal door behind her. Seconds later, the key clunked in the lock.

Beth had never felt so alone.

The pale green walls towered above her. She glanced up towards the high window where rays of the late afternoon sunlight broke through between the bars and cast shadows across the tiled floor. A single magpie sat on the windowsill and pecked at the glass. Her mother always insisted that magpies were a bad omen. That wasn't what she needed right now. She clapped her hands and shooed it away. It screeched and cackled as it flew off.

Beth reached for the box of items she'd been allowed to keep with her. She picked out the picture of Harrison dressed in his superman outfit. She'd taken it on her phone, just before they went to the nursery fancy dress party last month. Struth, was it only a month ago? It felt like a lifetime. Harrison was smiling that cheeky grin he always put on whenever a camera was pointed at him. He looked adorable. Thank goodness she'd had it developed; her phone, with all her other images of him, had been confiscated. She kissed Harrison's photograph and placed it on her bedside table. A sob caught in her throat and threatened to choke her. She swallowed, curled into a ball and burst into tears.

Eventually exhausted, her sobs subsided. She swung her legs off the bed and again picked up the photograph.

'Oh, Harrison, I miss you so much. I wish I could snuggle up with you, kiss your neck and make you giggle.' Her heart physically ached with longing.

She sighed. What had she done to deserve all this? So okay, she'd met Steve when both Maureen and Jan had told her to stay away from him, but did they expect her to live like a nun? Ron had abandoned her. She had her needs, and Steve was a good lover – or at least, he had been.

If only she could remember what happened. Why hadn't she stayed off the drink? But then, Maureen had been so insistent. Beth hadn't wanted to snub her, especially after she'd revealed such a tragic story and after she'd been so kind to Harrison.

And why were the police so determined to pin Steve's murder on her? Anyone could have arrived after she'd passed out. Anyway, surely, she could never have stabbed Steve. Could she?

All she'd ever wanted was to make a good home for Harrison and bring him up to enjoy the love she'd never had – a good start in life. How could that be so wrong? Her marriage to Ron hadn't worked out but, since moving in with Maureen, her life had been pretty well back on track. And now it had all gone belly up.

She put the photo back on the bedside table. This was no good; drowning in her sorrows wouldn't help anyone. After all, her barrister had sounded quite hopeful. He'd told her she might face a few months in custody until the trial, but he was confident he would get her off with a non-custodial sentence and that she'd be home before Christmas. She'd have to organise something really special this year, especially as she would miss Harrison's third birthday.

At least Harrison was being well looked after by Maureen. She *really* doted on him, more than his grandmother ever would. But then, what could she expect? No encouraging words had ever passed her mum's lips – they'd probably choke her. She was no doubt having a few "Oh Beth" moments since she'd been told about the arrest.

Who else but Maureen would take on the responsibility of looking after Harrison so responsibly? Thank goodness she'd had those guardianship papers prepared when she did. Beth owed Maureen big time for everything she'd done for them both.

Maureen opened her front door.

'Good morning, Mrs James. I'm Vic from next door. I've brought this letter. It came to us but it's addressed to Beth.'

'Thanks, I'll make sure she gets it.' Maureen reached out and took the pale blue airmail letter from her neighbour's hand.

'How's she doing? Any date for the trial yet?'

'I'm off to visit her next week, so I expect I'll know more then.'

'Give her my best wishes. Tell her I'm thinking of her. Poor little mite, I can't believe she'd hurt a fly. I've seen the way she dotes on Harrison.'

'Quite.'

'How is he? I bet he's missing his mum something awful.'

'We're all doing fine. Thanks for the letter.'

Maureen closed the door and returned to her armchair. She checked the monitor. Harrison was still asleep; she could hear his gentle snores. He'd been tired after his session at the playgroup that morning and had asked for his dummy and blanket straight after he'd eaten his lunch of pasta and grated cheese. She checked her watch; he'd probably sleep for another half an hour.

She concentrated on the letter. Who would write to Beth by airmail? She turned it over, and for the first time noticed the return address: *Mr R Taylor, HMS Kernow.* What was Beth's ex doing writing to her?

She walked into the kitchen clutching the letter, her thoughts in turmoil, and switched on the kettle. Holding the envelope close to the steam with one hand, she used her other to switch the kettle back on whenever it boiled. Eventually, she was able to peel the envelope open without ripping it.

Dear Beth,

How are you doing? Bet you're surprised to hear from me, but I've been thinking about you a lot of late. I miss you and Harrison so very much. Ever think about me?

I know our married life was less than ideal – let's face it, we fought like cat and dog, but I put that down to me being away so often. It must have been hard for you. And it was worse whenever we celebrated my shore leave with a drink. But you know what, I'm sure we could work it out? Especially if we stay off the booze, I haven't touched a drop for ages.

We didn't really give ourselves a chance, did we? Getting married so soon after we met. I knew I loved you, but we hardly knew each other. Then Harrison arrived six months after the wedding, bringing us so much joy, but also sleepless nights. It wrecked our sex life, which I'm sure you'll agree, was always pretty damn good. And who'd have thought a small baby could be so expensive? We were always short of money – no wonder you became so angry and violent. I should have been more understanding instead of running away as I did – fighting for good causes in the Caribbean instead of fighting for our marriage.

I know I don't see Harrison that often these days, only on my occasional shore leaves, but I've grown to love him so much. He's such a character. I have also come to realise that I still love you, despite our issues. Surely, we could give our marriage another try? If not for our sake then at least for Harrison's?

My commission comes to an end in September and I'll be free to leave the navy. I've got a good chance of finding employment at the docks in Falmouth. What do you think? Please write and let me know, and please send me an up to date photo of you both.

Much love, Ron. X

Maureen put the letter on the coffee table and shook her head slowly, as though in denial. She'd thought that Steve's death, and Beth's arrest for his murder, had eliminated any threat to her happiness. Now, it seemed, Ron wanted to return and play happy families. As Harrison's father, he would clearly have more legal rights to Harrison's custody than she did, especially when it was discovered that she'd lied to her solicitor at the time she'd commissioned the guardianship papers.

She couldn't even begin to think about life without Harrison. Bad enough that she'd lost Giles so young. Although, in the end that had been a blessing. The death of Anna and her unborn grandson had broken her. She'd found it impossible to recover from their loss, but then she'd met and fallen in love with Harrison. She'd do anything to prevent him from being taken from her – anything at all.

Perhaps she should simply destroy the letter and hope that Ron would give up. Even better; she would write *Gone Away, Return to Sender* on the envelope. That way he'd think that Beth had left the area. She reached for her pen.

# Chapter Eleven

Beth stood in the narrow corridor with the telephone receiver pressed tightly to her ear.

'Come on Maureen, pick up.' Even to herself, her voice sounded desperate.

The escort warder tapped Beth on the shoulder. 'Leave it, Beth. She's obviously not there.'

Beth shrugged her away. 'She has to be. She's not one for goin' out at night, *and* it's past Harrison's bedtime.' Relief washed over her as the phone was answered.

'Hello.'

'Maureen, it's Beth.'

'Sorry, I was in the shower.'

'How's Harrison?'

'He's fine. He went off to sleep about an hour ago. I read him *Room on the Broom,* which he loves. He usually stays awake until the end, but he was fast asleep by Page Five.'

Beth struggled to keep the panic from her voice. 'He's not ill?'

'He's tired. We walked to playgroup today. He refused to go in his pushchair – he says he's too old now he's nearly three. Then they did what he calls *'nastics'* in tumble tots before walking all the way back again. He'd already had a nap this afternoon, but he was still exhausted.'

'Listen up. I've only got a couple of minutes. You'll get a form in the next day or two. You need to sign it and send it straight back, so you and Harrison can visit in June.'

'Is that wise, Beth? Harrison knows you had to go away for a while, but he doesn't know you're in prison. A visit would upset him.'

'How?'

'He wouldn't understand why he couldn't stay with you or why you weren't allowed to come home with us.'

Beth's throat constricted. 'Please, Maureen. I need to see him. I'm goin' crazy here.'

'I'll think about it.'

'Maureen–'

The pips went. Beth screamed in frustration. She turned to the escort warder. It was Clare, the one who'd opened the door to A Block on her first day.

'Quick, Clare, give me another card.'

'You know I'm not allowed to do that.'

'Please. I have to speak to her before she fills in those forms.'

'Sorry, Beth, I can't help you.'

'Can't or won't?!' Beth snapped.

'Same difference.'

Beth pounded the wall with the palm of her left hand.

'Come on girl, get a grip.' The warder pulled the receiver from Beth's right hand and replaced it on the cradle. 'Let's get you back to your hotel suite.'

'But–'

'No buts. Get a move on. And don't be so bloody selfish. I've got others wanting to use the phone. Shift.'

Beth stumbled back to her cell. The door slammed behind her and the lock clunked. An hour later, the lights went out. After her busy days of scrubbing loos and floors, she usually fell asleep within minutes of the darkness descending, but tonight her mind was in chaos and she knew it would be impossible to sleep.

She thought back to earlier times when she'd taken Harrison to playgroup. He always enjoyed it, especially on the days Percy and Bea attended. They were his *bestist* friends. The three of them were Paw Patrol fanatics and would run around chanting – 'No job is too big. No pup is too small' – before collapsing on the floor in giggles. She missed that giggle. In fact, she missed everything about him, even his constant questions. She had sometimes rued the day he learnt the word 'why.' Now she yearned to hear him ask it – even if it was over, and over, and over again.

Maureen may be a saint, but she was no use at passing on information. Beth had rung her twice now, and written at least eight letters, but she'd only had one reply, and that was brief. Surely, after her own losses, Maureen would realise how much it hurt to live with this nothingness.

It was four long weeks now since she'd last seen Harrison, and she'd already missed so much. Maureen had told her that he no longer needed a nappy at night and could count to twenty, knew most of the words in *The Gruffalo* and would chant along with them as he watched the DVD. At this rate, he'd be at school before she saw him again and he'd have forgotten all about her.

Damn it, she'd meant to ask Maureen to buy Harrison that marble run game he wanted for his birthday. She'd write tomorrow; there was still time before his birthday next week.

Beth spotted Maureen, sat at the table in the far corner of the visitor's room. She rushed towards her, her heart pounding. 'Where is he?'

'He's having a nice day with Audrey, Bill's wife. You remember Bill, my friend the handyman?'

'He's not here? But you promised.'

'I promised to think about it, and I have, but I really don't think it's in his best interest.'

Beth collapsed onto the chair opposite Maureen, put her head in her hands and burst into tears. 'How could you do this to me?'

Maureen held out a packet of hankies.

'Here, Beth, have a tissue. Come on now. You know it makes sense. Prison isn't the place for children and he'll be well looked after. Audrey used to be a nursery nurse until she retired.'

Beth grabbed Maureen's hands and stared into her eyes. They were icy blue.

'Maureen, you *have* to help me.'

Maureen pulled her hands free, 'I am trying to help. I'm doing everything I can to make Harrison happy.' She reached into her shoulder bag and pulled out a brown A4 envelope. 'Perhaps this will help.' She pushed the package across the table.

Beth opened the flap and pulled out a couple of paintings and a colour photograph in a cardboard frame. The paintings both consisted of blobs and splashes of blue and green paint, with streaks of yellow. She wasn't sure what they were meant to be, but her heart melted at the thought of Harrison painting them. The photograph was of him holding a large birthday cake with three candles. He was wearing blue jeans and a checked blue shirt. Both were new. His eyes shone with excitement and his cheeky grin lit up his face.

'Dearovim.' Beth picked up the packet of hankies, took one, wiped away her tears and sniffed. 'Does he like the marble run?'

'I asked the shop assistant, and they said it wasn't recommended for youngsters under the age of four. It's not age-appropriate for younger children. There's a safety issue – they could swallow the marbles. I got him an Etch And Sketch, a popup book and some clothes instead.'

Beth stared at her, her heart pounding. 'But I promised. He'll think I've broken my promise.'

'I'm sure he won't. He'll have forgotten all about it.'

Had he already started to forget things she'd said to him? Would he soon forget her? He was no longer a baby, but at this rate it didn't feel like he was her little boy either. She knew she was being silly, but this twang of jealousy was difficult to push away. She swallowed and forced a smile; the last thing she wanted was to upset Maureen.

'Thanks. I must sound ungrateful, but I miss him so much.'

'I understand that, Beth. I really do, but you put me in charge of his care.'

Tears trickled down Beth's cheeks.

Maureen reached over and patted her arm. 'I'm only thinking of Harrison. I'm sorry, Beth, but his wellbeing has to be my priority.'

'What about my wellbeing?'

'You mustn't be selfish about this. Think of it from his point of view. How would we explain it to him?'

'Explain what?'

'Why you're locked up here in prison? Why you can't come home with us? Why he can't stay with you?'

'He's only just turned three. We could tell him I have to stay here for a while and that I'll be home soon. He won't know it's a prison.'

'As I said, I'll think about it. I really will, Beth. I'm honestly trying to do the best.'

Beth realised she should be grateful; she knew she should. And this conversation wasn't helping. She dried her eyes, blew her nose and looked around the drab visitor room. Four other prisoners sat at the small tables opposite their various visitors, heads close as they swapped news. She spotted June, a woman she often shared a table with over breakfast. That had to be her fiancé with her. June hadn't exaggerated; he was definitely fit. June had described how she constantly worried he'd be unfaithful while she was locked up. Beth had tried to sympathise with her, but her own pain got in the way. Beth wondered what June would do if he did cheat? She'd be stupid to let him break her heart, forgive him, and then spend the rest of her time here worried he'd do it again. Better to dump him and move on.

Beth jumped as Maureen spoke.

'Anyway, what news on the trial?'

'It'll be in October. Ridiculous, I'll have been stuck in this place, away from Harrison, for five months. How come it takes so long?' She looked again at the photograph. 'Three – he's no longer a baby. What new words is he using?'

'You would have laughed the other night. He was watching *Paw Patrol* on Netflix and I told him it was time for bed. He said, "Oh no, Nana Mo, just one more episode."'

'*Episode?* That's awesome. What about playgroup, does he still love it?'

'He misses Bea, now she's started nursery. But I've promised him he'll join her in September. I sent his application in.'

'What?'

'An application for a nursery place in September.'

Beth's stomach felt as though she'd swallowed a bowl of live worms. 'Where?'

'St Charles's.'

'Isn't that one of those God schools? I don't believe in all that crap. Why didn't you check with me first?'

'Well, Bea will be there. I knew you'd agree it was best, you know, for him to be with his friends.'

How dare Maureen take over like this? She wanted to scream at her: *he's my son. I should decide where he goes to school.* But of course, she couldn't take the chance of upsetting her. She must simply sit there and smile her agreement, even though her stomach continued to churn. She had to hold on to the fact that Maureen was doing an excellent job looking after Harrison. Without her, Harrison would be in foster care or a home. She swallowed. 'Of course, you're right. He'll love being back with Bea.'

A smile played across Maureen's lips. Beth wanted to smack her.

'I know this is difficult for you, Beth. I'll send you some more photographs, but I'd best be off now.' Maureen glanced at her wristwatch. 'It's too far for me to drive all this way, so I came by train. There's one due in half an hour.' She stood and picked up her shoulder bag.

'Please, say you'll bring him next time, Maureen.'

'I've told you, Beth. I'll think about it.'

Beth watched Maureen's progress as she crossed the room. She waited, expecting her to turn and wave goodbye, but she left without a backward glance. Beth had always thought that Maureen offered them a home because she was fond of them both. Now it seemed she may have been a bit naïve. It was all about Harrison. For the first time, she was seeing the other side of the coin, as Maureen always liked to say.

Maureen took her coffee through to the lounge and sank into her armchair. Phew. At least she had a few hours to herself while Harrison was on a trip to Newquay Zoo with his playgroup. She'd volunteered to go with them, but Susan, the manager, told her they had enough help, although she was welcome to join them if she really wanted. Maureen decided a few hours rest might be preferable to trudging around the zoo with a gaggle of three-year-olds; she got tired just looking after one.

The phone rang. How annoying.

She put her coffee cup onto the table and walked through into the hall. 'Hello?'

The line went dead.

How rude! Couldn't they apologise if they'd dialled a wrong number? That was the trouble these days; people were in too much of a hurry to remember their manners. Perhaps it was one of those scammers she'd heard so much about? Preying on old-aged pensioners and emptying their bank accounts. The scammers wouldn't get her money, no way. Every month she withdrew her pension payments the day after they were paid in, reducing the bank balance back down to fifty pounds.

She sank back in her chair and picked up her coffee. The doorbell rang. What now? She put down her coffee and went through into the hall and opened the door.

'Oh hello. Is that my grocery order? I was expecting Mr Price.'

'He's got a bad cold. He asked me if I'd deliver for him instead.'

Could you carry them through to the kitchen table? I'll get you your money? How much do I owe you?'

'Forty-five pounds and fifty pence, please. We had to swap milk chocolate buttons for your order of Milky Stars, I'm afraid. We haven't had any delivered from the wholesalers this week. Out of stock, apparently.'

'That's fine, go through to the kitchen, I'll be with you in a tick.'

Back in the lounge, she grabbed a key from the pocket at the side of her armchair, unlocked the bureau and took out a Clark's shoe box. After removing fifty pounds in crisp ten-pound notes, she hurriedly put the box back, turned the key in the lock and returned it to the side-pocket of her chair. 'Here you go,' she said as she entered the kitchen. 'I don't have the correct money, I'm sorry.'

'No worries, Mrs James. I have change.'

He handed over her money and she walked him back to the front door.

'I'll ring through with my order next week, as usual. Thank goodness you do these home deliveries. I don't know where I'd be without you.'

'That's alright, Mrs James. We small shops have to make our money any way we can these days. It's no bother.' He waved as he descended the steps.

Maureen returned to the kitchen. She'd better put the ice cream in the freezer immediately. The rest could wait until after she'd finished her coffee. At least Mr Price wasn't at all bothered about her paying cash, unlike that stupid woman in the fudge shop.

She'd been impressed with the display in the shop window. The fudge looked very appetising and the gift wrap packaging was very pretty. This was just the sort of thing she was looking to get for Audrey's birthday present. Maureen was well aware that Audrey had a sweet tooth; her matronly figure demonstrated the fact only too well.

Maureen entered the shop, triggering a musical tune as she walked across the doormat. She was engulfed by the heavenly sweet smell of the merchandise. It made her mouth water.

A young girl rushed through an open doorway at the rear of the shop, her long blonde ponytail swinging from side to side as she stepped behind the counter and smiled. 'Can I help you?'

'I'd like one of those gift-wrapped packages of fudge you have on display in the window, please. The plain clotted-cream kind. It's for my friend's birthday. She likes nuts, but the last thing I would want is for her to crack a tooth on a Brazil nut and finish up at the dentist.'

The girl picked up a packet from the shelf behind her and pushed it across the counter towards Maureen. Her slim fingers were dressed with several silver rings and ended with long fingernails, each one perfectly shaped and painted a different colour and pattern. Maureen registered the Union Jack, polka-dots and stripes before she realised the girl was waiting.

'Have you got a bag, or do you want a 5p carrier?' the girl asked.

'I'm fine, thank you. How much is that?'

'Four pounds and fifty pence, please.'

Maureen pulled out her purse and took out the correct change.

'We don't take cash.'

'What?'

'Only debit or credit cards.'

Maureen stared at the girl. 'I don't have either. I don't believe in such things. How can a shop not take cash? That's ridiculous?'

'It's safer and saves a lot of time and costs. We don't have to cash up at the end of the day, or take the money to the bank.'

'But surely you must lose customers?'

'Why would that be? Everyone has contactless these days.'

'Well, you've lost my custom. Let that be a lesson to you.'

Maureen pushed the package back across the counter, turned on her heels and stormed out of the shop.

Don't take cash! Whatever was the world coming to? It was like the supermarkets, and even W.H. Smith, taking out sales personnel and putting in these stupid self-serve swipe and pay desks. They'd soon learn. People wouldn't stand for it. She wouldn't stand for it.

She pushed the ice cream into the already packed freezer draw, and then rummaged in the shopping bag, until she found the box of fudge, she'd ordered from Mr Price. There, Audrey would have her present after all, paid for in cash.

# Chapter Twelve

Hi Jan,

Wish you were here – no really, I do. You'd help me sort my head out. I think I'm going crazy.

I miss Harrison every minute of every day. I'm desperate to see him. Can you bring him? Maureen promised she'd think about it, but I don't think she will. In a way, I sort of get where she's coming from – she reckons it would upset him – but once he's here I'm sure I could handle that.

I going to send you a form, so you can book a slot to visit me next month. Don't worry about Maureen. I'll write to her and tell her you've got my permission. Please say you'll do it. I know I'm asking a lot, but there's no one else I can trust.

Beth

Hiya Beth,

I've filled in the form and sent it back, so it should be with the prison's administrator well before the 20th July. In plenty of time for us to get our pass. I've contacted Maureen. She tried every trick in the book to persuade me that bringing Harrison wasn't a good idea, but she eventually agreed.

Let me know if there's anything you want me to bring – other than Harrison, obviously. See you later.

Jan


Beth's heart raced as she ran towards the visiting room.

'No running in the corridors!' Clare shouted.

Struth, this was like being back at school. 'But, Clare. I don't want to miss a minute.'

'You'll miss more than a minute if you don't do as I say.'

Beth slowed to a quick walk and entered the visitor's room. She saw Jan immediately and looked around for her first sight of Harrison. Every day, since her arrest, she'd dreamt of holding him in her arms again. Would he have grown? She rushed over to Jan.

'Where is he?'

'At home with chickenpox.'

'No!'

'Oh, Beth, I'm so sorry. I know how much today meant to you. I wasn't sure what to do, but I thought I'd better come anyway.'

Jan grabbed Beth's hands as they both sank onto their seats on either side of the small table. Tears poured down Beth's cheeks. She struggled to breathe. As if she'd been punched in the stomach.

She shook her head. 'I don't believe it.'

'No, I couldn't believe it either. It's so unlucky.'

Beth looked at Jan. 'No, I mean, I don't believe it. She's lyin'. I know it.'

'Oh Beth, surely not? I know it must be hard for you, but Maureen clearly loves Harrison to bits. I bumped into one of your neighbours this morning. She said what a great job Maureen was doing, taking Harrison to playgroup, the beach and keeping all his routines going.

Of course, Jan was right. Jan was always right. Beth sniffed. 'You're always the sensible one, as my mum would say.'

'I went to see your Mum,' Jan said.

'Yeah, I'm sorry I dumped that on you.'

'I didn't mind going. She was a bit shook up, but you know what she's like. Always quick to condemn. Blamed your father – whoever he was. Said it was his genes. Blamed you too, said you were stupid to mess things up with Ron when he was such a good catch. Too good for you, she said. I got quite cross with her at that point. I told her it was her lack of love, affection and encouragement that made you the way you are.'

'You didn't?'

'I did. Though I don't think it sank in.' Jan shook her head.

'While I think of it,' Jan said, 'the neighbour also told me that she took a letter round to Maureen last month. She thought it was from Ron, said his name was on the back. Did Maureen bring it in to you?'

'Ron? What would he be wantin'?'

Jan frowned. 'You didn't get it then?'

Beth shook her head slowly. 'No, I didn't.'

Jan frowned again. 'Why wouldn't she pass on your mail?'

'Probably, for the same reason she won't bring my son in to see me, and the same reason she wouldn't let you bring him today. I know, I know, chickenpox, but she's lyin', I know she is.'

'It must be easy to get paranoid, stuck in here.' Jan put her hand on Beth's arm and squeezed. 'I did get to see him, you know. Just briefly, over her shoulder. He was standing at the door of the lounge, clutching his blanket, with blotches of calamine lotion on his face and arms. I said hello to him.'

'What did he say?'

'He said, "I'm poorly." I didn't say anything about coming to see you. I didn't want to upset him.'

'I'd give anything to see him and share a cuddle.'

'Well, I didn't exactly get to cuddle him. Maureen wouldn't let me in, said chickenpox was highly contagious. I told her I'd had them as a kid, but she insisted you could get them twice, or it can come back as shingles.'

Beth frowned. 'Anybody can dab a few blobs of calamine lotion on non-existing spots, and Harrison always says he's poorly when he's just tired. Oh, Jan, what can I do?'

'Well, stop crying for the first thing. I know you're upset but crying will only give you a headache.'

'What would you do?' Beth pleaded.

'I'm not sure. You're between a rock and the proverbial as far as Maureen's concerned. You need someone to take care of Harrison, and she's doing that. But if she lied about the chickenpox then…Only, I don't understand, why would she?'

'Well, think about it. With me stuck in here, she's in charge. She wants Harrison to forget all about me. She wants me to rot in here.'

'Look, like I said, Beth, crying's not going to help. And no matter how much Maureen might, or might not, want you locked up in here, it won't be up to her, will it?'

'I don't know what to do.'

'Then do nothing. Harrison's perfectly safe where he is. You need to concentrate on your case, on getting yourself out of here. After that, well, you can shove Maureen back in her bloody box, can't you? You're Harrison's mum. He belongs with you. Right?'

'Too bleddy right,' Beth said.

The bell rang to alert everyone that visiting time was over.

'Let me know if there is anything I can get you. Or do.' Jan gripped Beth's hand tightly, reached over the table and hugged her. 'Chin up, darling. You'll get through this.'

'Come on, you lot! Let's be 'aving you!' Clare stood at the door. 'Chop, chop!'

Beth walked towards the door. She noticed Clare's BO hadn't improved. She tried not to breathe as she walked past her into the corridor that led to A Block.

The cell door clunked behind her, the key turned in the lock and her heart sank. All she had of her son was the odd photo, while Maureen got him all to herself. But what could she do about it, stuck in here?

Maureen switched off the TV and picked Harrison's blanket up from the sofa. 'Come on, mischief. Let's get you in the bath.'

'Don't want to.' His bottom lip pouted as he snatched the blanket from her.

'We can get all that calamine off you. You'll feel much better. Come on, it's not like you to sulk.'

'You sent Jan away. I like Jan. She made me ducks.'

'Yes, but you were poorly weren't you? You'll feel better after a bath, and then you can get into bed and I'll read you a story.'

'*Room on the Broom*?'

'If you like.'

She gripped his hand and led him up to the top floor. She'd moved her bed up here with him since Beth's arrest. It was easier and quicker if he cried out in the night, which he did quite often these days. She ran the bathwater, added some bubble bath and Harrison's yellow plastic ducks.

'Do you want your potty? Here, let me help you with your trousers.'

'I can do it.'

He struggled out of his trousers and pants, pulled his T-shirt over his head and sat on his potty.

'Finished.'

'Good boy. You don't want to wee in the bath, do you?'

'That would be naughty,' he giggled.

She lifted him into the bath and crouched down to sponge the calamine away. 'There we go, all better.'

'Harry not poorly?'

'Not now, Harrison. It's playgroup tomorrow. We don't want to miss that, do we?'

Harrison reached for the ducks, lined them up in a row and started to sing. '*Three little ducks went swimming one day.*'

Maureen joined in. '*Over the hills and far away. Mother duck said, quack, quack, quack, quack, but only two little ducks came back.*'

'When my mummy come back?'

'Soon, darling. She'll be back soon.'

'I miss Mummy.' His eyes filled with tears and a couple rolled down his cheeks. He sniffed and wiped his nose with the back of his hand.

Maureen flinched. 'I know you do, pet. But you've got me. You love Nana Mo, don't you?'

'I love Mummy best.'

Despite having her arms in warm soapy water, Maureen shivered. 'Let's get you out, into your pyjamas and off to bed. Then I'll read you your *Room on the Broom.*' She draped the towel over his shoulders and lifted him out of the bath. 'Ouch.'

'What matter, Nana Mo?'

'You're such a big boy now, and I'm not as young as I was.'

Was she really up to all this? Her sciatica was a great deal worse and she was absolutely exhausted. Being in charge of a three-year-old, twenty-four hours a day, seven days a week, was much more difficult than she'd imagined. Perhaps Beth would be acquitted and they could return to the situation they'd enjoyed before. But then, she'd be back to worrying constantly that Beth would meet someone and move out. Why was life so complicated?

Beth walked into the canteen. The hubbub of noise and chatter alerted her to the fact that she was later than usual. She had a shocking headache – Jan had been right about that – and getting her act together had taken longer than normal.

She picked up her tray and walked over to the table where June sat. June looked rough; perhaps she was coming down with a cold. Beth put her mug of tea and bowl of cereal on the table, picked up her spoon and leaned the tray against her chair leg.

'I didn't see you at visiting yesterday. What happened to Romeo?'

'He's dumped me.'

Beth looked across at June's red eyes, swollen nose and bloated face. She realised now that it was a night of tears that had caused the devastation, not illness. 'Oh, June. I'm so sorry.'

'He said it was like serving a prison sentence himself.'

'Sounds a bit selfish.'

'No, it was because he knew how worried I was about him meeting someone else that he stayed in all the time. It's my jealousy that's pushed him away.'

'I know what you mean. I feel the same, in a way, about Maureen. If I criticise owt she's doin' or lose my rag – either because she refuses to bring Harrison to see me, or makes a decision I should have made – then she could stop sendin' me any news.'

Beth poured the small jug of milk over her muesli. 'What will you do about your ex?'

'I suppose I'll wait until I get out and hope he's still single. If I dress up and go to see him, I might be able to tempt him back. What would you do?'

'I'd dress up, go out and find someone else who's a bit more reliable.'

'Is that what you did when you split up with your husband?'

Beth laughed and shook her head. 'Perhaps you'd best forget my advice. That's exactly what landed me here. Out of the fryin' pan and into the fire. Or rather out of one violent relationship and into another.'

June finished her tea while Beth gobbled down her cereal. 'Do you still speak to your ex?' June asked.

'Ron? He's often away, but he visits whenever he's on shore leave. He still wants to be a part of Harrison's life. He usually takes him out for a McDonalds.'

'Couldn't he help?'

'How?'

'No idea, but he could act as a link between you and Harrison, couldn't he?' June picked up their trays and put the empty mugs, bowls and cutlery on them.

'He's no idea I'm here, or about what's happened.'

'Perhaps you should tell him? After all, he is the father of your child.'

Beth watched June walk across the canteen and put the trays in the racks. Perhaps she had something there. Ron might be able to help, if it was only by keeping an eye on Harrison – and Maureen. That had to be better than doing nothing, didn't it?

# Chapter Thirteen

Beth opened the air-mail letter. Her hands shook as she unfolded the thin paper and saw Ron's familiar writing.

Dear Beth,

I was pretty gutted when my first letter came back *return to sender*. I thought you'd decided you wanted nothing to do with me. I can't understand why Maureen didn't pass it on. Especially as you tell me she's been so kind to you, what with giving you a home when you needed one, and looking after Harrison while you're away.

You don't need to worry that I'll think less of you because you were seeing Steve. I abandoned you, I don't blame you at all. Please believe me when I say that I still love you and realise now that I was an absolute fool to treat you the way I did. I blame myself. You being charged with murder would never have happened if I hadn't walked away from you and Harrison. I'm so sorry and will understand if you find it impossible to forgive me, but I am determined to spend the rest of my life trying to make things up to you both.

Let me explain how I discovered just how stupid I've been. I became friends with the ship's medic, George Adams. I don't usually discuss my private business with anyone, but one night we were ashore in Barbados, drinking the local spiced rum, which has an awful effect of loosening the tongue, not to mention the brain addling headache it produces the next day. He asked me if I was married, and I told him about you and Harrison. I told him how beautiful you were, how much I loved you both and what a good mother you are.

He couldn't understand why we weren't still together, so I explained how things came to a head between us after a series of horrific fights and how, when you attacked me on that last occasion, I'd decided I couldn't stand the violence anymore and signed up for a year away on hurricane relief work in the Caribbean. I can still remember your words that day. *'If you walk out on me now, don't bother coming back.'*

I think by this stage of the evening I was fairly maudlin and went on to tell him how I could never understand why you got so violent on a glass of wine, or at most two. He got quite excited at that and reckons that you have something known in the trade as Pathological Intoxication, or Alcohol Idiosyncratic Disorder.

Apparently, it's quite rare. He's pulled off a description of it for me. It's described as – *an unusual condition that occurs when a small amount of alcohol produces intoxication that results in aggression, impaired consciousness, prolonged sleep, transient hallucinations, illusions and delusions.* He says that these episodes can occur rapidly, may last for several hours, and are usually followed by total amnesia.

I couldn't sleep that night. The very thought that your violence might actually have been caused by an illness kills me. I should have known something wasn't right and supported you, rather than run a mile. I treated you so badly, especially as you were struggling to raise our son at the same time as you had to cope with my absence, or rather desertion. I'm so ashamed.

I can't believe you finished up being evicted from our flat and living in that hostel? How did that happen? The first thing I knew about it was when your mother wrote to me to say you'd left the hostel and moved to the flat in Falmouth. I was so pleased to see Harrison again when I next visited that I forgot to ask about the hostel.

Write to me and let me know all the details about your arrest, and why the police are so convinced it was you that murdered this guy. What can I do to help? I'll do anything.

Thinking of you, Ron, X

Her hands shook as she read his letter over and over again. Her mother was right about one thing – the man was a saint. He'd taken her thing with Steve on the chin, and he wasn't attacking her as an unfit mother, even though she was about to go on trial for murder. He wanted to help her.

She wiped her eyes with her sleeve. Fact was, what could he do? Nothing. But he wanted to try, and she wanted to let him.

The last week had dragged by. Every day she had hoped for news of Harrison, but nothing came. Then, this morning, she'd been handed a letter. At, first, she'd expected it to be from Maureen, but no, it was a pale blue envelope from Ron. She'd saved it for when she was back in her cell. She sat on her bed and ripped the letter open.

Dear Beth,

You poor darling. I don't know how you're managing to cope, either with being separated from Harrison or with life cooped up in that prison cell. Especially when I remember how much you used to enjoy being outside in the fresh air. Remember our walks along the beach? We would watch the tide come in and listen to the seagulls as they circled above us, screeching, swooping and diving to warn us off if we strayed a bit too close to the rocks where they'd built their nests.

I wish I could swoop in and rescue you from that cell of yours and whisk you away to where I am now, in St Lucia. It was our last day in port yesterday so we were granted shore leave. We'd all been working double shifts to get the ship ready for the crossing, so the captain treated us to a day off. I spent the day with George, the medic, exploring the island from a catamaran. We sailed around the Pitons – they look like huge green pyramids – and then visited the sulphur springs at Soufriere. I couldn't help thinking about you as we walked through the botanical gardens. There's a beautiful waterfall, which featured in the film *Romancing the Stone*. Little pathways meander through amazing plants, such as birds of paradise and orchids. It was almost like being at the Eden Project and nearly as humid. I even spotted several hummingbirds. I'd love to bring you back here one day if you'd let me. I know you'd love it and I still owe you a honeymoon.

Inevitably the conversation returned to you and your predicament. Please don't be cross with me, but since I got your letter explaining the murder charge, I've been trying to think about how I could best help you. I asked George's advice and I do believe he's come up trumps. He believes that this Pathological Intoxication, or Alcohol Idiosyncratic Disorder, could be used as your defence in the murder trial. Apparently, it is well documented in the *Diagnostic and Statistical Manual of Mental Disorders* and can, therefore, be used as a defence in a case like yours.

You told me you had wine with Maureen prior to you going out with this Steve, and don't remember anything even before getting into his car. George is convinced that this demonstrates that you are a classic example of this disorder and that you'd have been unable to form any sort of rational judgement. According to him, you would be unaware of your actions and totally incapable of making a decision to kill or cause grievous bodily harm to anyone. He's convinced that you would be acquitted of murder. You will, however, still be liable to a charge of an unlawful act of manslaughter, but hopefully, as a mother of a young child, the judge wouldn't send you back to jail, but instead issue you with a non-custodial sentence.

George has agreed to be a witness at your trial, unless your lawyer can find an expert witness to testify. Please write back to me and give me permission to make an appointment with your legal team to discuss this line of defence. Please let me help you.

I'm also sorry that my abandonment led to you becoming homeless. I was appalled that the landlord turned up and made a pass at you. No wonder you let fly at him. And what a bastard he was, issuing you with an eviction notice and reporting you to Social Services like that. You must have felt truly deserted and blamed me, quite rightly. As I told you in my last letter, I am so sorry for the way I treated you. I still love you and hope you will eventually be able to forgive me. I want to be a better father to Harrison and help to give him the life he deserves.

We are sailing back this evening and I will spend the rest of my time in the navy, until I leave in September, based in Devonport. I know now that you never got my first letter because Maureen sent it back, *return to sender*, but I'm thinking of applying for a job in the Falmouth Docks. I know you like Falmouth and that way I'll be close to you both, even if you can't find it in your heart to forgive me (which would be entirely understandable). Let me know what you think.

Lots of love, Ron XX

Beth blinked back the tears. Ron knew she'd had an affair with Steve and that she could be guilty of murder and yet he was still offering to take her back and make a home for her and Harrison. No wonder her mother had described him as *bleddy rich*. But did she love him enough to commit to this life he was proposing? Surely, she had, once upon a time? She'd been terrified he'd drop her when she'd told him she was pregnant but was that because she loved him, because she didn't want to lose him, or because she was frightened of bringing up a baby on her own? Had she even thought that through? And, yes, he was quite right: she'd felt abandoned when he'd cleared off to the Caribbean for a year. But she blamed herself for driving him away.

One thing for sure: she needed to send him the authority to speak to her barrister, and she would also send him the forms for him to visit her at the next opportunity, which would now be in August. Maybe things would be clearer by then. She would also ask him to visit Harrison, perhaps take him out and make sure everything was as it should be. It would remind Maureen that Harrison had a mum – and a dad – and that she couldn't make changes to Harrison's life without checking with them first. Now, she just had to find a way to survive the next few weeks.

At least she'd been moved away from toilet cleaning. She was still cleaning in the mornings but had now advanced to the administration corridors. In the afternoons, she worked in the prison library. She really enjoyed her new role; it had inspired her to start reading again, something she hadn't done since she left school. It helped to pass the time while she was alone in her cell. Ironically, a good murder mystery could help her to escape the prison walls and forget her own loneliness and misery. She picked up her latest book and began to read.

Maureen smiled as she opened the door. 'Do come in Mr Taylor, take a seat.' She indicated the lounge door and then waved him towards the armchair opposite hers. As he walked past her, his aftershave wafted over her. It smelt wonderful, obviously very expensive. He clearly took full advantage of his duty-free opportunities.

'Please, call me Ron.' He perched in the chair. 'Thank you for agreeing to see me at such short notice, Mrs James.'

'Maureen. Call me Maureen, please.'

'Is he here?'

'Taking a nap. He should wake up soon, but I always find it best to let him sleep it out. I'd rather not wake him just yet. Tea?'

'I'm fine.'

She sank into the armchair facing him. 'You're on shore leave I take it?'

'My ship's docked in Devonport for a few months. Having a paint job. I was granted a couple of days off to come to Falmouth because I had an interview at the docks. I've just been offered a job as a senior engineer. I start in September.'

'Congratulations.' Maureen forced a smile.

'Don't say anything to Harrison yet, but I'm hoping to persuade Beth that we should get back together and make a home for him.'

Maureen felt the blood drain from her face. So, this was how they planned to repay her for everything she'd done for Harrison. How dare they?

'Lovely, I'm sure,' she said.

She shifted her position, sitting up straighter in an attempt to ease the pain in her leg.

'But don't you think you need to take things more slowly – one step at a time? You don't want to be upsetting Harrison any more than he has been already. Anyway, where would you live?'

'It's early days yet, but I'm thinking of buying one of the new homes being built at Goldenbank. I hope, eventually, to persuade Beth we should get back together and that it will become our family home.'

'They won't be ready for September. And in any case, if you take Harrison away from me, who will look after him when you're at work? Beth's court case won't be until October, and we can't be sure she'll get off without a custodial sentence.'

Ron frowned. 'We have no intention of taking Harrison away from you. You'll always be a part of his life, as far as we're concerned. You're his much-loved Nana Mo, after all.'

'But if you buy a home for you and Beth, you'll take him to live there...with you?'

'Well obviously, that's the plan. But you would still see him at weekends, some evenings. You might even have him stay over so that Beth and I could go on date nights now and then. If you want to, that is?'

Maureen stood. 'I think I can hear him moving, I'd best go up.'

'I'll go.'

'No! He's not expecting you to be here. It would be a bit of a shock to wake up and find you in his room.'

Maureen rushed into the hallway and climbed the stairs. The pain in her sciatic nerve was throbbing today, but it was nothing compared to the searing pain in the centre of her chest at the thought of Ron and Beth betraying her.

She peeped through the doorway into Harrison's bedroom. He was sitting up in bed, rubbing his eyes. His hair was all rumpled and damp. She walked to his side and ran her fingers through his hair, bent over him and kissed the top of his head.

'Up you come, Harrison. You have a visitor.'

'Who?'

'Let's go down and see, shall we?'

Harrison raced down the stairs, into the lounge and threw himself at Ron. 'Daddy, Daddy.'

Maureen felt a surge of jealousy. He hardly ever saw his dad, and yet this display of affection was far more than she'd ever been rewarded with, even in the early days when she'd only seen him for their weekly coffee and cookies.

Ron picked him up and cuddled him, before sitting him on his knee. 'Gosh, you've grown. It must have been that McDonald's we had last time I was here.'

Harrison giggled. 'Silly, Daddy. I'm three now – I'm a big boy.'

'So you are. Do you want to go to the beach and have an ice cream?'

'Yes!'

'Manners, Harrison,' Maureen said.

'Sorry, Daddy. Yes, please.' Harrison ran into the hall and came back with his shoes.

Ron sat him on the chair and knelt to put them on. 'I was thinking about what you said, Maureen – about taking it slow – and perhaps you're right. Do you know of anyone who may be renting out a room or a bedsit? If I could find one nearby, it would mean that when I start work at the docks in September, I'll be close enough to see Harrison every day.'

The cheek of it! Ron obviously expected her to offer him Beth's room, but if he thought she'd allow him to stay with her while he cooked up his family reunion plans – well he could think again.

'I'll ask around,' she said.

'Thanks, Maureen. Come on then, buddy!'

'He has his tea at five.'

'Don't worry. We'll go for a McDonalds.'

Maureen watched from her front window as Harrison and Ron walked down the steps and along the pavement. She felt an overwhelming sense of loss as they disappeared around the corner. Her eyes filled with tears. How dare they? After everything she'd done. Expecting her to live off tit-bits from the table with visits on occasional week-ends and a sleepover when they fancied a *date night*, whatever that was supposed to mean. Sex, probably. Well, this family reunion simply wasn't going to happen. She'd make sure of that.

# Chapter Fourteen

Jane, the warder who'd escorted Beth to her cell on that first day, stood in the hallway leading to the visitor's room.

'Nice tan, Jane,' Beth said. 'Was your holiday abroad?'

'Two weeks in Morocco. Pure bliss. Is that Adonis waiting patiently in there your ex-husband?' Jane opened the door to the visitor's room and nodded to the far side, where Ron stood with a huge soppy grin on his face.

'Sure is. Although, he's tellin' me that the ex-part is under review.' Beth smiled and walked towards him.

He wrapped his arms around her in a bear hug and rocked her from side to side, before pulling back to kiss her on the cheek. 'I've missed you so much, let me look at you.' He grabbed her hands and together they sank onto the hard-wooden chairs on either side of the small table. 'You look good.'

Beth's heart rate raced as she looked into his eyes. She could feel the hairs on her arms bristle and her stomach lurch. She hadn't felt like this since the early days of their relationship.

'I've got so much to tell you,' Ron said. 'Not sure where to start.'

'Tell me about Harrison. How's he doin'?'

'I've only had the chance to see him the once so far – the day I had my interview – but I've spoken to him on the phone a couple of times. He's such a star, a real character, very bright and so polite. You've done a wonderful job bringing him up. I can't wait until September. Only a couple of weeks now. I'll get to see him every day. And I'm longing for the day you come home and we can all be together.'

So, he was still planning a reunion, despite everything she'd done – or might have done. Could this really happen for them? Harrison would be so happy if they could make it work. He didn't get to see Ron very often, but there was no doubt that he loved his dad.

'How's Maureen? Is she still doin' a good job lookin' after him?'

'I'd say yes and no. She cares for his every need, keeps all of his routines going, makes sure he goes to playgroup so he gets to socialise. He still goes to gymnastics, swimming and does lots of walking, so he's pretty fit.' Ron frowned and ran his hand through his hair. 'My only doubt is about how obsessive she is about him. She even asked if we'd "take him away from her" if we get back together.' He took her hand and kissed her fingers. 'We will get back together, won't we?'

Beth looked into his eyes. They burned brightly with an intensity she had never noticed before. Her stomach fluttered and her eyes filled with tears.

'Hope so.' She realised her voice was low and husky.

Ron smiled and gripped her hands more tightly. 'I've been to see your legal team and I took George with me. They're pretty excited about this pathological intoxication line of defence. Your lawyer is coming to see you next week, but they're already preparing along those lines. I've given them a statement about some of the fights we had, how violent you became after only one – or at most two – glasses of wine, and how you always passed out and couldn't remember anything the next day. Jan has agreed to act as a witness to previous episodes you've suffered when she's been with you. And, believe it or not, so has your mother.'

'Strewth, what did you say to her? She's never offered to do owt for me before.'

Ron grinned. 'You know how she adores me, for some strange reason.'

'Tell me more about Harrison. What did you get up to?'

Beth rested her head in her chin as she listened to him describe his afternoon out with Harrison, smiling at the thought of Harrison squealing on the swings, balancing along the low wall of the park pretending he was a circus act and then the meal at McDonalds.

Jane clapped her hands together. 'Ten minutes, folks!'

Beth glanced across the room. Only two other prisoners and their visitors were here today. One was Hilary, who it was rumoured had buried her father in the garden so that she could continue to claim his pension. Her visitor, presumably her husband, was a strange-looking little man in a beige raincoat, with a pointed nose and black horn-rimmed glasses. He reminded Beth of a rat, especially the way his nose twitched. They weren't holding hands or leaning close together to speak, but sat stiffly and spoke very little.

The second woman was unknown to her, a recent admission, probably enjoying the ritual of toilet cleaning that the newbies always endured. Her visitor was an elderly woman. They bore a slight resemblance, probably her mother. The younger woman wept while the older one patted her hand and dished out paper handkerchiefs.

Ron leaned over the table and kissed her gently on the forehead. 'I'll write to you, often, but I won't get to see you again until the trial. I start the new job next month, so I won't be able to get any time off, but I'll be thinking of you. Oh, I nearly forgot...' He pulled out a folded paper from his jacket pocket. 'I've brought you this to look at.'

Beth glanced at the papers and frowned. 'What is it?'

'House details, currently being built in Goldenbank in Falmouth. I'd welcome your opinion?'

'Why?'

'Well, it's about time I got onto the property ladder. And one day, hopefully soon, I hope to persuade you that it will be a good family home for the three of us. They won't be ready until next summer, but I'll need to put a deposit down in the next couple of weeks. Write to me and let me know what you think.'

'Promise me you'll spend as much time with Harrison as you can. And...give him a big hug and a kiss from me.' Tears rolled down her cheeks.

Ron brushed them away. 'I've advertised for a bedsit or small flat from September, so that I can be near to Harrison. I'll try and see him every day and I promise to take him out lots.'

'I don't see why Maureen can't let you stay in my room – miserable cow.'

'Best not to rock the boat by even asking at this stage. I made it pretty clear I wanted to be local, but she never offered. I think she wants to keep Harrison to herself for as long as possible. Hopefully that won't be for much longer.'

The bell rang. Ron pulled her to her feet, wrapped her once more in a bear hug, picked up his jacket and turned to leave. As he walked towards the exit, he glanced over his shoulder several times, until he was ushered out through the door by Jane.

Jane closed the door on all three visitors and then returned to escort the women back to their cells.

'He's keen that one,' Jane whispered to Beth as they walked back. 'And drop dead gorgeous. Don't be letting him go.'

'I'm beginnin' to believe he's a keeper. Anyhow, I don't think my mother would ever speak to me again if I messed up this time.'

'Good luck, Beth.' Jane opened the cell door and ushered Beth inside. 'Sweet dreams.'

Beth lay on her bed. Perhaps she could begin to share Ron's plans for the future. She picked up the papers Ron had given her. It was a lovely home; only small, but it had three bedrooms, a nice sized garden and it was handy for town. Ron would be home in the evenings every day. They would have weekends as a family. And when Harrison was at pre-school, she could probably get a part-time job herself, perhaps at the library?

Sweet dreams indeed.

She picked up her latest book: Agatha Christie's, *A Caribbean Mystery.*

Time was passing so slowly. It seemed ages ago now since she'd seen Ron, although, in reality, it was only three weeks. She looked at his latest letter. A white envelope, date stamped Falmouth. His sailing days were definitely over, just as he'd promised. She tore it open.

Dear Beth,

Good news. I've managed to get a tiny bed-sit near to the docks, just around the corner from Emelia Boulevard. So I'm now able to see Harrison every day after work and every weekend. Obviously, he'll sleep at Maureen's still. My place is too small and also, I had to sign to say I wouldn't have guests.

Not sure Maureen's too happy about seeing Harrison so much less, but there you go. Actually, she'll suffer a double whammy because he starts pre-school next Monday, three days a week.

I'm glad you like the look of the house in Goldenbank. Hopefully you'll like it even more when it's finished.

I started my new job this week. Nice group of lads and the work's quite varied. I'm working on a ferry at the moment. I think I'm going to enjoy it here. I certainly love seeing Harrison every night and especially looking forward to our first weekend together.

Unfortunately, I won't be able to get down to see you this month. We work flexitime, but I will need to save up any hours I get so I can get some time off for the trial in October.

You must be feeling very nervous about the whole thing, but I'm confident that even if you are found guilty, they will take the pathological intoxication into account, as well as the fact that you are the mother of a young child, and will issue you with a non-custodial sentence. You'll be out by the end of the day and we can all go for a celebratory meal. Probably at McDonalds if Harrison gets his way.

Love you very much, XXXXX from both of us.

# Chapter Fifteen

Beth shrank into the corner and sank to the floor. The cold, damp wall chilled her back. She raised her hands to her head and squeezed, but the pulsating throb continued. Tears streamed down her face, dribbled through her fingers and fell to the tiled floor. How had it all gone so wrong?

She glanced around her surroundings. The small cell stank of disinfectant and had no windows or furniture apart from an uncomfortable looking bench. The female guard, who'd escorted her down here from the witness box, had left five minutes before, locking the door firmly behind her as she left.

As she'd left the courtroom, her lawyer, Neil, had whispered to her that he'd be down shortly, to discuss what had just happened. But for now, she was alone.

She reached across to the wooden bench beside her and hauled herself onto it, sniffed and wiped her tears away with the sleeve of her blouse. What *had* just happened? And, more to the point, *how* had it happened? She had been fairly optimistic as she ate her lunchtime cheese and tomato sandwich and gulped down a mug of tea. It was Day Two and the trial was going so well. That morning, the medical specialist, John Banks, had explained pathological intoxication. Beth could see from the way the members of the jury leaned forward in their seats, that they were fascinated by his explanation.

The prosecution barrister tried his best to explain how difficult the illness was to identify: no blood test being available to verify its existence...how prone it was to forgery by someone who can act...how difficult it is to reproduce the effects under controlled conditions... But, on the whole, Beth thought the jury appeared reasonably satisfied – at least they were nodding in all the right places.

Her defence barrister introduced her witnesses: Jan, Ron, her mother and that creepy landlord, David Smith. He explained that David Smith had initially refused to give evidence and was, therefore, summoned to the court as a hostile witness.

Ron, Jan and her mother all testified in turn that they had witnessed the extreme reaction she demonstrated after consuming small quantities of alcohol and how she became angry and aggressive before losing consciousness for several hours. Each of them also confirmed that she would have no recollection of her behaviour or of anything that happened while she was affected. Beth cringed as her mother told the court how, on one occasion, she'd pulled down the welsh dresser in the dining room and smashed every precious piece of her mother's pottery collection. They weren't valuable, but they'd meant a lot to her mother. At the time, Beth had felt guilty, but her sense of guilt soon evaporated as her mother continued to demonstrate far more concern for the broken knick-knacks than she ever did for Beth.

David Smith explained how he'd visited Beth to negotiate a payment plan for her rent, which in arrears. He'd taken a bottle of wine as a demonstration of his friendship and reasonableness. He described how she had welcomed him in, shared the wine and then became extremely aggressive towards him. He admitted, under questioning by the defence, that he may have tried to kiss Beth, but claimed she was *'up for it'* and that he had no choice but to serve her with eviction papers – even though this would inevitably make her homeless. Beth's defence asked him if he felt guilty about putting a young mother and baby out on the street, to which he had replied: 'I told Social Services I was evicting her because she was in arrears and had been extremely violent. Not fit to look after a young child in my opinion. It was their responsibility to make sure they had somewhere to go. In any case, she asked for it after that black eye she gave me. I had a hell of a job explaining that to the wife.'

The prosecution then explained that the steak knife used to murder Steve had no other fingerprints apart from Beth's. They also claimed it had been taken from Maureen's house and that this indicated that Steve's murder was pre-meditated.

Beth's barrister nodded at her and smiled reassuringly. He'd explained this whole knife business. According to him, the prosecution was clutching at straws.

He rose to his feet. 'Objection! The knife, while of the same type as those found in Mrs James's house, could have come from a myriad of sources.'

Her barrister then called the area manager for Wilkinson's to the stand. She testified that approximately four-hundred sets of these stainless-steel sets with imitation bone handles had been sold in Cornwall. They were, in fact, very common. He went on to make the point that Beth had no motive for murdering Steve.

Beth remembered nothing from when she got into Steve's car and could not, therefore, be found guilty of murder but only of manslaughter due to her diminished responsibility. The only possible explanation, her barrister suggested, was that Beth, before she met Steve, had imbibed two glasses of wine while she was with Maureen and that this had resulted in a pathological intoxication episode.

The barrister for the prosecution leapt to his feet, shouting. 'Objection! Conjecture!' The judge agreed. Too late, the point had been well made.

At this stage it was all going swimmingly, her barrister was smiling broadly and Beth dared to believe in his confidence. He'd predicted that she would receive a non-custodial sentence and be home by the evening – back with Harrison, where she belonged.

And then the prosecution called Maureen to the stand.

'Mrs James, I believe the accused and her three-year-old son, lodged with you?'

'Beth did stay with me for about three months until she was arrested for murder in May. Since then I have been looking after Harrison. I am his legal guardian.'

Beth's stomach had cramped. Bleddy hell, did Maureen really have to mention the word *murder* at this point?

The barrister smiled at Maureen. 'A big commitment for you I'm sure.'

'Oh, he's no trouble.'

The barrister handed her an A4 sized photograph. 'Could you look at this picture? Do you recognise the steak knife?'

Maureen nodded. 'It's mine. One of a set of six.'

Beth stared, unable to believe her ears. What was going on?

'And how can you be sure it is one of yours and not one belonging to another of the four hundred sets sold locally?' The barrister looked across at Beth's defence team and smiled.

'Because it has a crack in the handle.' Maureen pointed to the photograph. 'Just here. Can you see it?'

Beth's breath caught in her throat. She shook her head. Had she heard right? Confused she looked at Ron, he looked so pale. Then she looked at her barrister. He was shaking his head and rifling through the papers in front of him. What the hell was happening?

The jury members studied the photograph. A low murmur ran through the courtroom.

Her barristers face had turned grey, his expression stony. He sat very still.

Why didn't he do something? Why didn't he object? What the hell was Maureen playing at?

The prosecution barrister glanced around the courtroom and smiled. 'And how do you think the knife ended up at the victim's home?'

At last, Beth's barrister sprang into life. 'Objection, you are asking the witness for an opinion.'

'I apologise, Madam.' The prosecution barrister bowed to the judge before returning his attention to Maureen. 'When did you last see this particular knife?'

'I tend not to use it for eating in case the handle splits, but I thought it would be alright as a letter opener. So, I used this one to open the envelope of legal papers I wanted to show to Beth before she went out. They included my will, naming Harrison as my beneficiary, and the legal guardianship papers, which she signed.'

'That was very generous of you, Mrs James. Harrison is your sole beneficiary?'

Maureen nodded. 'He inherits everything, apart from a couple of small cash donations to charities, yes.'

The barrister paused and picked up the photograph. 'So, when did you last see this knife?'

'The last time I saw it was just before Beth went out that night. It was on the coffee table next to Beth's wine glass and handbag.'

'Hm, I understand you enjoyed some wine together that evening.'

'I'm so sorry; I never knew Beth had a problem with alcohol. I don't have wine these days very often and I thought it would be nice to enjoy a couple of glasses with Beth – to celebrate the legal papers being signed off.'

The barrister looked over at the jury and smiled. 'Another kind gesture, Mrs James. Did you know Beth was meeting the victim that night?'

'She told me she was meeting her friend, Jan.'

'So, the accused lied to you?'

Maureen looked across at Beth and frowned. 'It seems as though she did, yes.'

Beth glared at Maureen. What was she doing? Her testimony couldn't be any worse if she was deliberately trying to cause trouble.

Someone in the jury coughed and muttered an apology.

'Thank you. That will be all.' The barrister for the prosecution took his seat and shuffled his papers noisily, straightening them into a neat stack.

Maureen held Beth's gaze, smiled, and then turned away to step towards the back of the witness box.

'Please wait, Mrs James,' the judge said. 'Does the defence have any questions?'

Beth's team leaned together into a huddle. Her barrister stood and looked across at the judge. 'No thank you, Madam. No questions.'

'Mrs James, you are free to go.'

The prosecution and defence teams summed up their evidence and then the judge sent the jury off to deliberate.

Two security guards led Beth back down to the small holding cell. Another official brought a tray containing three mugs of tea.

Beth gripped her mug and thought back over Maureen's evidence. She knew Maureen would be compelled to tell the truth, but she appeared to be enjoying her role and even making the evidence look as bad she could. Was that deliberate, or simply the result of a clever prosecution team? Would this make a difference to the outcome? Had Neil been too optimistic about her being home with Harrison by the end of the day.

Her thoughts went back and forth, one minute believing she'd be released, the next, terrified she'd be sent back to jail. Her rollercoaster of emotions continued until, three hours later, there was a knock on the door and the message delivered that the jury was coming back. She put her cold mug of tea back on the tray and trailed, handcuffed between the two security guards, back to the witness box.

The foreman of the jury was asked if they had reached a decision on the verdict. They had. Not guilty of murder, but guilty of manslaughter because of Beth's diminished responsibility while suffering from an episode of pathological intoxication.

Beth gave a huge sigh of relief. She whispered her thanks to the jury.

The judge recapped on all of the points made during the trial. Beth wondered if all this wittering would ever come to an end. Eventually the judge finished her summing up and came to the point of announcing the sentence.

Beth stood in the dock, her legs like jelly, her heart racing. She looked up into the visitor's gallery, where Ron stood. He still looked pale, but smiled at her. Maureen stood beside him, ram-rod straight with an anxious frown.

'You have been found not guilty of murder, but guilty of manslaughter by reason of diminished responsibility during an episode of pathological intoxication.' The judge looked at Beth over the rim of her glasses and then returned her gaze to her papers. 'The sentence can range from seven years in custody, down to a deferred sentence.'

Beth glanced back at Ron, who now had a faint smile on his face. He looked so handsome. And he'd been so supportive over the past few months, especially by identifying this line of defence and spending time with Harrison. Perhaps this was the chance they needed?

The judge turned over her papers. 'I am satisfied that the prosecution has shown that the steak knife used as the murder weapon was taken from the home of Mrs James, and that the only fingerprints on the knife were those of the accused. Therefore, the only person who could have taken the knife to the murder scene was the accused.'

Beth's stomach sank. She could feel the heat spread across her cheeks. She could sense Ron staring down at her, but couldn't bear to look at him.

'I am also satisfied,' the judge continued, 'that the accused has testified that she remembers nothing after meeting up with the victim, *even before* getting into his car. We only have her word for that. No witnesses have come forward who can throw any light on when this pathological intoxication episode began, or even took place, although I accept the jury's verdict on this. However, she must have picked up the knife and put it in her handbag *before* leaving home. I therefore find that the actions of the accused, in taking the knife to the scene, contributed to the victim's death. Beth Taylor, I sentence you to five years in prison.'

Beth heard a chorus of gasps from the gallery, before the world went black and she slumped to the floor. The next thing she knew, the female security guard and her lawyer were helping her to her feet.

The keys rattled in the lock and she looked up as Neil was ushered into the cell.

'Beth, what can I say? This is so unexpected.' He opened his arms wide.

She pushed herself up from the bench and fell into them, sobbing. He patted her back until her sobs subsided.

'Five years! I can't do it! Harrison will be eight before I ever see him again. He'll forget all about me.'

'Come now, it won't be as bad as that. We'll appeal. And if that doesn't work, you'll get time off for good behaviour.'

Beth pushed herself upright. 'Appeal? When can we do that? How long will it take?'

Neil steered her over to the bench, held her arm while she collapsed onto it, and then sat beside her.

'We have to seek permission for an appeal, firstly with this judge, and if she won't grant it, with the Court of Appeal. It will take several months, but the main stumbling block is that we need to have a reason to appeal – or new evidence.'

'Like what?'

He patted her hand. 'Well there's the problem. What possible new evidence could we find? We will need to put forward something that proves there has been a miscarriage of justice. At this point, I have to be honest with you, I have no idea how we will do this, but I can assure you, I will do my very best. I'll start by looking at past cases, see if we can find evidence of the judgement being unnecessarily harsh.'

Beth's head was spinning. She thought she was about to be sick, but swallowed the bile that rose in her throat.

'I have to go now. I have a meeting with your barrister, and your husband asked if he could see me. But I'll visit you in the next couple of days to discuss the way forward. They'll be here shortly to take you back to prison. The same place for now, but we may be able to get you moved to a more open prison if we can prove you're not a danger to the public or at risk of absconding.' He looked at her with a slight frown and shook his head, slowly. 'That bit may be more difficult.' He hugged her, before tapping on the door to be let out. 'See you soon. Chin up, my dear.'

The door slammed behind him.

# Chapter Sixteen

Maureen hung her coat up and kicked off her court shoes. Court shoes. She chuckled. How appropriate. She put them into their designated space within the settle, pulled out her slippers and slipped them on. Slipping on the slippers. She chuckled again. Now all she needed to do was settle on the settle. This time she laughed out loud, before picking up the handset and dialling Audrey's number.

'Hello, Audrey. I'm back now if you'd like to drop Harrison around? I would've called in, but I wasn't sure if he'd be eating his tea.'

'Maureen, my dear. Have you seen the news? It's in today's edition of the *West Briton*, so it must be true. M&S in Falmouth is to close next year, during the first week of February.'

How could that have happened? Maureen had written to the Chief Executive Officer when the rumours first circulated. Didn't he realise how important it was to keep the branch open? Where would she buy her underwear from if this was allowed to happen?

'I'll write again. They must have misplaced my letter.'

'How silly of me,' Audrey said. 'I forgot it was the final day at court today. How did it go?'

'She got a five-year custodial sentence.'

Audrey gasped. 'However will you manage?'

'I suppose I'll have to advertise for a cleaner.'

'No, I mean with Harrison. I know he's a delight – I've really enjoyed his company today – but he's such a handful. Especially at our age.'

Our age? How dare she? Audrey had to be at least five years older than her – overweight, very unfit. She always arrived at Maureen's front door out of breath after climbing the steps.

'I'll manage just as I have for the past few months. If he's worn you out, you'd better bring him back right away.'

'I'll be round in a few minutes. He's just finishing off his ice cream.'

Maureen tutted. Ice cream? He'd want it every dinner time now, instead of it being a special treat.

She replaced the receiver, wandered into the lounge and sank into her armchair. She sighed deeply. Today couldn't have gone any better. Five years of Harrison, all to herself – well, except for Ron sticking his nose in at the evenings and weekends. She hadn't even needed to use the escape route she had prepared just in case. She wasn't going to have the two of them arriving on her doorstep and depriving her of Harrison. It simply could not happen. She smiled to herself, as she thought back over her brilliant plan.

She'd spotted the advert for the cottage in the agent's window two years before. She recognised it immediately as the one she knew from her childhood and had collected a copy of the details. It was a nice memory. She'd kept it in the bureau until earlier last month when she suddenly realised that she might need a plan, just in case the court issued a non-custodial sentence, as Ron was predicting. She had rung the agent to enquire about the cottage's availability and was thrilled to find it was free until Easter. The only drawback was that the six-month rental would be four thousand pounds. It seemed a lot of money at the time, but then Harrison was worth every penny if it meant she could keep him with her. At least there had been plenty to cover it in the shoebox, where she kept her cash savings safely locked away in her bureaux.

The rental agency was only a short detour after dropping Harrison off at nursery school. The woman on the reception desk had been aghast when Maureen had handed over the full rental amount in twenty-pound notes. She'd even had to check with her manager to make sure it was okay to accept it. They'd expressed some concerns about the possibility of counterfeit notes or money laundering, until she'd explained how she always paid for everything in cash and that she didn't even own a credit or debit card. Fortunately, they'd eventually accepted the cash, but they'd insisted that she return the following day to collect the key, once the money had been safely cleared by the bank. The key had been on her key ring ever since. Should she cancel the rental now it wasn't needed?

The doorbell rang. Maureen jumped up and rushed to the door.

'Come in Aud…Oh!' Her hands shook as she opened the door wider and forced a smile.

'Come in, Ron. I was expecting you to call later this evening. Let's go through to the lounge and take a seat. Would you like a cup of tea?'

She realised her nerves were making her gabble. She took a deep breath and willed herself to slow things down.

'I don't want tea, but I do need an explanation.' Ron perched on the edge of the sofa. 'Sit down, Maureen.'

She sank into her armchair. 'I'm sorry about this afternoon, but I had to tell the truth.'

'Why are you claiming to be Harrison's legal guardian?'

Maureen blinked. She thought he might challenge her about her testimony, but she hadn't been expecting this.

'It's true. I am his legal guardian. Beth signed the papers. And thank goodness she did! What would have happened if I hadn't given him a home?'

'How did you get the legal papers signed without my permission? You're not Harrison's legal guardian while Beth's away. I am. You'd need my authority as well as Beth's to assume that role.'

'But you're separated.'

'Not legally. And, as you know, we're working on that. I double-checked with Beth's lawyer, and there is no way your solicitor should have produced those papers without my involvement.'

She flinched under his glare. Ron had never been anything but softly spoken before now. She could feel Harrison slipping from her grasp; she simply had to find a way to calm him down.

'I'm sorry…It must have been a mistake.'

'I can take Harrison away at any time I choose, Maureen. Do you understand?'

So, he wasn't threatening to do it yet. Her pulse quickened. There was still a chance she could rescue this. She nodded, looked at the floor and shuffled her feet.

'I'm sorry, I was only thinking about Harrison's best interests.'

'Don't get me wrong, Maureen. We're very grateful to you for everything you've done for Harrison. But I want you to understand, he is our son and our responsibility. Do I make myself clear?'

She could feel the colour inflame her cheeks. How dare he speak to her like a naughty child? She wanted to strike back, remind him again how much they owed her, but she couldn't take the risk.

She sniffed and pulled a tissue out of her pocket. 'I'm sorry if I've caused you any distress.'

Ron reached over and touched her hand. 'You know we appreciate everything you're doing. You've been wonderful with Harrison. We couldn't have managed without you. Now I need to see him. Where is he?'

'He'll be home shortly. Audrey looked after him while I was at the court. I rang her to let her know I was home, so she'll be here any minute.' She frowned. 'Are you going to tell him his mother's been found guilty of murder?'

'Well, I don't expect I'll be quite as blunt as that, but I may have to explain some of it. Even though Beth is going to appeal, it will still be a few months before she comes home.'

Maureen's heartbeat raced. 'Appeal? On what grounds?'

'I don't know yet. I spoke to her lawyer after he'd been to see her. Apparently, although she's taken it all rather badly, she's determined to fight on. If nothing else, we'll challenge the verdict as being unnecessarily harsh.'

Maureen looked up as the doorbell rang. 'I think that must be them.' She dashed to the door. 'Come in, Audrey. Afternoon, precious. Your daddy's here.'

'Daddy!' Harrison ran into the lounge and threw himself into Ron's arms.

Ron lifted his son high over his head and kissed his tummy. Harrison giggled.

'Audrey, we'll go through to the kitchen, have a cup of tea and a catch up while we leave these two young men to do the same.'

'Can't stay, Maureen.' Audrey said. 'I have to get back and put Bill's dinner on. Sorry to hear about Beth's sentence, Ron. You must be very disappointed.'

'Devastated more like, but she's going to appeal.'

'Good for her. Sorry, Maureen, must dash.'

Maureen closed the front door behind Audrey and stood in the lounge doorway watching Ron and Harrison play. They were oblivious to her existence. Harrison hadn't even said hello. 'I'll get his dinner ready.'

Ron put Harrison back down on his feet and stood. 'No thanks, Maureen, I'll take him out for something to eat.'

'But-'

'I'll have him back before bedtime.'

Maureen stood at the open door and watched as Harrison and Ron descended the steps. Her eyes prickled with unshed tears. What if he didn't bring Harrison back? He would, wouldn't he? Surely they still needed her?

She made a determined effort to keep her voice steady. 'Bye, Harrison. Have a nice time.'

Harrison turned around and waved. 'Bye, bye, Nana Mo. See you later.'

She closed the door firmly, walked back into the kitchen and grabbed the kettle. Maureen's head raged with the unfairness of it all. Her life had been ruined by injustice. Bad enough losing Giles at the ridiculous age of thirty-eight and especially those awful few weeks before he died, but the loss of Anna and the unborn child had been unbearably cruel. She'd died herself that day. Since then she'd only existed, day after endless day, until that tiny bundle of joy, Harrison, had swept her off her feet on the entrance step to the diner café. And now they planned to appeal, get back together and take Harrison away from her. They had no right to take Harrison away and deprive her of the only pleasure she'd experienced since Anna and her baby grandson had died.

She could feel the rage building, the hard knot of fury in her chest causing her pulse to race and her head to throb. She'd pay them back for this somehow, just as Anna's husband, Tony, and her husband, Giles, had been made to pay. She made herself a cup of tea and sat at the kitchen table as she thought back to that week, seven years ago.

She'd also been sat at the kitchen table that day, enjoying a cup of tea, when the doorbell had rung. She wondered who it could be. Mr Price had already delivered the groceries that week and she wasn't expecting anyone else. She glanced at her watch. A bit late for visitors. The bell rang again.

'Okay, okay I'm coming.' Maureen had opened the door and almost fainted. 'My God, Anna, whatever has he done to you? Her daughter stood on the top step, her hair unbrushed and straggly. She was wearing a coat with a torn sleeve. Her face was bruised, she had a black eye and a split lip.

Maureen opened the door wide. 'You'd best come in.' She closed the door behind her, led Anna through into the lounge, waved her towards the sofa and sank into her armchair. 'I didn't expect to see you again. I thought you'd made your bed.'

'Mum, I'm so sorry we had words. Please forgive me.'

'You defied me. You promised me you'd take up your place at university and wait until after your degree was finished before you married that lump of no-good.'

'I loved him.'

'Mm, and look where that's got you.' Maureen pointed at Anna's eye. 'Walk into a cupboard door, did you?'

Anna had stared down at her feet. 'He often hits me, but this time was the worst yet.'

'And what do you expect me to do about it? I begged you not to marry him, but you chose to betray me and elope.'

'I sent you several letters to apologise, but you never replied. I rang you often, but you never answered. Do you hate me that much? I never stopped loving you.'

'It's too late now. You should have listened to me at the time.'

'Please, Mum. I need your help.' Anna stood and shrugged off her coat.

Maureen looked at her daughter's swollen belly. 'Oh, my God, you're having a baby?'

'I'm eight months pregnant. It's a boy.'

Maureen had rushed over to Anna and threw her arms around her. 'A grandson, Oh, Anna. How absolutely wonderful. I always wanted a boy.

'I'm so worried Tony's going to harm our baby.'

Maureen's heart thundered in her chest. 'That's not going to happen,' she told her daughter. 'Just let me think. Sit here a minute. I'll make us some tea.'

A few minutes later, she returned to the lounge and put the tray on the coffee table. She smiled at Anna, poured milk into the cup, added tea and handed it to her.

'You need to get away from him, Anna.'

Anna cradled her cup in her hands and ignored the tears running down her face. 'I've been trying, Mum. but I've nowhere to go.'

'We could turn the top floor into a flat for you and my...your son,' Maureen said, hardly daring to breathe as she waited for a response.

Anna stared at her. 'You'd do that, Mum? After everything?'

Able to breath at last, Maureen shrugged. 'I could put a kitchen in the back bedroom, and the front bedroom could be your lounge. That way you still have the two bedrooms and a bathroom, so we wouldn't have to live in each other's pockets. I could even get Bill to put a front door on the landing, so it's like a separate apartment.'

'Oh my God, that would be amazing.'

'You can stay in the spare bedroom until we get it all sorted.'

'I don't deserve you, Mum.'

'Yes, well...' Maureen sipped her tea. 'I was thinking...about the baby, you could call him Harry, after my grandfather.'

Maureen was only five when her grandfather died, but she could still remember how kind he was. A wonderful man.

Anna smiled. 'Why not?' She leaned forward and put her cup down on the coffee table. I have to go back first. I need to tell Tony I'm leaving. I owe him that.'

Maureen couldn't believe what she was hearing. 'You can't go back to that animal. He could hurt you... and...Harry.'

'I've got all my stuff to pack. Could you pick me up on Saturday morning?'

'I'm not sure about this. Why don't I go back and pack? You stay here and rest.'

Anna shook her head. 'Please, Mum. Try and understand. I can't just walk out. I need to talk to him.'

'But-'

'Mum, I have to go.'

Maureen could see that Anna was determined. 'Right.' She picked up their cups and stacked them on the tray.

'I'll get Bill in first thing. But if it's not quite ready we'll muddle through until it's finished. Do you need a lift home?'

'I've got the car. Tony's out with his mates for the evening. They collected him an hour ago.'

Maureen picked up her pen and notebook from the side pocket of the chair. 'Here, you'd better write down the address.'

Anna gave her the details and a spare set of keys. 'Come about nine, he'll be out by then. There's an away match. Use the keys if I don't answer the door straight away. It takes me forever to get down the stairs these days.'

Maureen kissed her daughter's cheek, careful to avoid the bruising. She walked Anna to the door and watched as she struggled down the steps, clambered into her car and drove off.

Foolish girl, why hadn't she done as she was told? At least something amazing had resulted from her betrayal:

a baby boy, Harry, to love and cherish. The chance of a new life to make hers worth living again.

No one had responded to her knock on the door. She'd been surprised, expecting Anna to meet her on the doorstep, bags packed and ready to leave that no-good husband of hers. She should never have let her return to Tony the other night, but at least now he'd never get the chance to knock her around again. Using the set of keys Anna had given her, she let herself in, walked through the hall and into the kitchen.

Her heart thudded as she caught sight of Tony. He sat at the kitchen table, head in his hands, tears running down his cheeks and splashing onto the table surface: drip...drip...drip. He'd looked up as she walked towards him.

'This is all your fault!' he snarled.

'What are you doing here? I thought you were at football. Where's Anna?'

He jerked his thumb in the direction of the stairs. 'You did this.'

Heart racing, Maureen ran up the stairs and into the bedroom where Anna lay on her side, her eyes closed. Poor darling, all this emotion at this stage in the pregnancy couldn't be good for her, or the baby. She had to be exhausted. 'Come on darling, time to go.' She slipped off her gloves and stuffed them in her pocket, then leaned over and stroked Anna's hair out of her eyes. Anna's forehead was icy cold. Maureen's stomach lurched. 'Anna. Anna, wake up!' Maureen shook Anna's shoulder. She didn't respond.

Maureen knelt at the side of the bed and felt Anna's neck, checking for a pulse. There was none. Maureen's head spun. Tiny white lights floated before her eyes. The room darkened. She clutched the bedside table and waited for the fainting threat to pass. She tried to stand, staggered, bumped into the dressing table and fell back against the door. A scream escaped from her. She could feel her pulse race and flutter with palpitations. Steadying herself, she clung to the doorframe until her vision cleared and her pulse slowed.

Dead. Her darling girl was dead. And so, therefore, was her grandson. This could not be happening. It had to be a nightmare. Any minute now she'd wake up and they'd still be alive. The baby had been a promise of her new start in life.

Should she dial 999? Could they save Harry?

Of course they couldn't. If she'd arrived at the moment Anna had died, and CPR had been applied, then perhaps. But Anna's skin was cold; she must have died some time ago. There was no hope for any of them.

Maureen stumbled back to the bed. She leaned over and gently kissed Anna's forehead.

'Sleep in peace, my darling girl.'

She placed her hand on her daughter's stomach.

'Goodbye, Harry. How will I live without you?'

She turned and walked from the room, grabbed the handrail and descended the stairs, slowly. She reached the kitchen door from where she could see Tony, hunched over the kitchen table, his shoulders shaking. He looked up as she stepped closer.

'She's dead, isn't she?'

She stared at him. 'You killed her.'

'No. I admit we argued. But she had an asthma attack and collapsed.'

'Did you ring for an ambulance?'

'No point.' He ran his hand through his hair and looked up at her. 'I knew she was dead. It was her fault. She was leaving me – stupid cow.'

He hadn't even tried to save her. 'They could have saved my grandchild!'

Tony sneered. 'What? Save a brain-damaged kid?'

Maureen saw the carving knife. It lay on the kitchen table, its black handle pointed invitingly towards her. She pulled out her gloves and slipped them on, picked up the knife and moved towards him.

'Put the knife down, Maureen. You'll hurt yourself.'

Maureen thrust the knife into his chest. The blade sank in about three inches before she let go of the handle and stepped back. She remembered wondering if that was deep enough to pierce his heart.

Tony's eyes widened in surprise. He grasped the knife with both hands, slumped forward and then, as though it was happening in slow motion, dropped to his knees. Maureen could feel the blood draining from her face as she watched Tony topple forward. The knife handle hit the kitchen floor. His body collapsed on top of it. A pool of blood seeped out from under him and trickled, like a crimson stream, across the pale grouting towards her.

Oh, my God! What had she done? She reached down and felt for his pulse. For the second time that day, she failed to find one. Anger flared through her. Death was too good for him. He should have suffered – *really* suffered. But then…at least this way Anna and the child had been avenged. He'd taken everything that mattered to her, and now he'd paid.

She snatched off her gloves and shoved them back into her pocket. At least she wouldn't have left any fingerprints on the knife. She reached for the phone and dialled 999.

Yes, Tony had deserved to die.

Maureen picked up her cup and saucer, washed them under the tap and wiped them dry with her tea towel, before stacking them away in the cupboard.

Anna had suffered for her betrayal, she'd made sure Tony had suffered for his, and she'd damn well make sure that Ron and Beth suffered too.

She wandered back into the lounge and sank into her chair. She couldn't concentrate sufficiently to read her book. She'd just sit here and wait for Harrison to return. Ron would bring him back, wouldn't he? Of course he would. Harrison belonged with her. Even Ron knew that, deep down.

# Chapter Seventeen

Beth hung back as the other inmates rushed into the visitor room, eager to see their loved ones. She couldn't face him, not now. Not after he'd been forced to give evidence about how violent she could be – or after he'd sat through the evidence given by that creepy landlord.

David Smith was right: she wasn't fit to look after a child. Harrison was better off without her. They both were. Ron was probably only here today to tell her that he'd changed his mind. There'd be no more talk of them getting back together.

'Come on Beth, where's your get-up-and-go gone? Dreamboat's waiting for you in there.' Jane stood in the doorway; she held back the door to usher Beth through.

'Take me back to my cell, please?'

'I can't do that. You'll have to wait 'til visiting's over, and you can't stay here on your own, so you may as well go in.'

Beth's eyes filled with tears. 'It's best if he forgets all about me. Him *and* Harrison.'

'From what I gather he's working damned hard to get you released. He wouldn't do that if he didn't still love you. Don't lose heart, Beth.' Jane pushed the door wide open. 'Now, get on in there.'

Entering the room, Beth spotted Ron. He looked anxious but he smiled as she walked towards him and then frowned.

'Gosh, Beth. You look...'

'Guilty?'

'So thin. Have you eaten anything in the last two weeks?'

'I lost my appetite.'

Ron reached for her hands. 'My poor darling. What can I do to make things better?'

Beth shook her hands free, sank onto the uncomfortable chair and pulled out her handkerchief. She brushed aside a tear that was threatening to dribble down her cheek and sniffed. 'Nothin.' Unless you can explain how, and why, Mad Mo turned everyone against me like that.'

'Not everyone, Beth. I still love you. Always will. And so does Harrison. And Jan. Even your mother, although granted, she has a strange way of showing it sometimes.'

'Maureen will turn Harrison against me. He'll never want to see me again.'

'Nonsense. He talks about you all the time. He's always telling me how he loves you to the moon and back.'

Beth put her elbows on the table and covered her face with her hands. Her shoulders shook. The lump in her throat threatened to choke her. She gasped for breath. 'But...she's with him all the time. I haven't seen him for months.' She scrunched up her handkerchief and scrubbed her eyes. 'We need to get him away from her.'

'I spend every evening and weekend with him. And don't forget, he's at pre-school three days of the week now, so he spends a lot less time with her. I honestly believe that although she's weird, obsessed even, she does look after his best interests.'

Beth glared at him.

'Come on, Beth. Try not to get too worked up about it. You'll make yourself ill.' He reached for her hands again and clutched them tightly. 'I did put her right on this nonsense about her being his legal guardian.'

'I'm such a bleddy idiot. Why did I sign those papers?'

'I checked with your lawyer. Her solicitor should never have drawn those papers up. Not without my involvement. In your absence, I'm still Harrison's legal guardian and I've made sure she knows that.'

'She tricked me,' Beth spat the words out. 'And then she tricked the judge somehow. If it wasn't for that bleddy knife I'd be home now. I can't even remember takin' that knife with me. Why would I?'

'You're my wife, Beth, the mother of my son. I promise you I'll do everything I can to get you out of here. I just need something to go on. Where should I start?'

Beth sighed. 'Okay, you're right. Let's start with the things we can prove. Could you go and see her solicitor, threaten to report him or somethin'? Get him to explain why he did those papers without you knowin'.'

'I'll ring for an appointment, first thing tomorrow, promise.'

Beth squeezed his hand. 'Thanks, I should never have been so stupid. What was I thinkin'?'

'You were thinking about Harrison. Please, Beth, don't beat yourself up. How could you have known?'

'But you knew.'

'Well, I studied some law as part of my engineering degree. Not family law, obviously, but enough to make me suspicious.' Ron smiled. 'I'll write and let you know how the meeting goes.'

'There's something else you can check out for me.'

'Name it.'

'I was desperate to see Harrison, still am, although what the hell I'd say to him now, I don't know. Maureen kept makin' excuses, but Jan agreed to bring him in to see me, back in July. It was all arranged. But when she went to collect him, Maureen said he had chickenpox. She lied. I know she did. I thought that if we can prove she's dishonest, it might perhaps help the appeal?'

'Okay, but how?'

'You could go to his old playgroup, see if they have any records of him being off, or having chickenpox.'

'I'll go on Wednesday. It's my early night. I finish at three so I'll be able to get there before they close.'

Beth shivered as Ron stroked the back of her hand. A slight frown creased his suntanned brow, but his eyes twinkled as he continued to smile at her. She could tell he still loved her, adored her even. 'I was afraid of seein' you today. I thought you'd blame me and that you'd agree with David Smith about me being an unfit mother.'

'No way. You're a perfect mum. We just need to get you out of here and back home with us both. Start our lives as a family over again.'

'You still believe in us?'

Ron leaned towards her and kissed her forehead. 'Even more so.'

'You didn't believe David Smith sayin' I was "up for it?"'

'That creep? I didn't take any notice of his crap, and nor should you.'

Tears trickled down her cheeks. Ron took her handkerchief from her clenched fist and gently wiped them away.

It was impossible. She'd be stuck in this hell hole for at least another two years. Harrison would have forgotten all about her. She'd never get to share that special bond with him ever again, and Ron was bound to meet someone else. An icicle of fear pierced her heart as she realised that she really didn't want that to happen.

'Five-minute warning folks!' Jane shouted across the room. 'Start wrapping up!'

'What do you want me to do about Harrison? Should I take him away from Maureen?'

Every nerve in her body tingled. She wanted to say yes, and as quickly as possible. However, Ron's studio flat was unsuitable. The school run would be difficult now that Ron was at work, and the two days that Harrison wasn't at school would mean new child care arrangements. To move him at this stage would unsettle and upset him, and that wasn't really fair. After all, Mad Mo wouldn't actually cause him any harm. She loved him far too much for that. She sighed. 'No. Leave things as they are for now, but keep a very close eye on her. And don't let him forget me, or how much I love him.'

Ron stood, pulled her to her feet and kissed her cheek. 'Please try and eat something. We need to keep our strength up – all of us do. I'll write and let you know how my sleuthing goes and I'll be back next month for a visit – hopefully with better news.'

'Give Harrison a big kiss from me.'

Beth struggled to stop more tears from brimming over as she watched Ron cross the room. He turned and blew her a kiss. She pretended to catch it and place it over her heart. She didn't deserve him. How long would it take for him to realise that?

# Chapter Eighteen

Beth ripped the letter open. Her hands shook. Had Ron found proof of Maureen's lies?

Dear Beth,

First of all, good news: I saw Maureen's solicitor who was flabbergasted when I explained who I was. I demanded to know why he had drawn up guardianship papers for Maureen, without my permission. He said Maureen had told him I'd been killed on active duty. I felt quite sorry for him as the colour drained from his face. After all, he had no reason to doubt her. He apologised profusely and admitted he made an error – he should have asked to see the death certificate. He told me the guardianship document was invalid, even if we were separated, which we aren't – well anyway, not legally. While I was with him, he rang your lawyer to explain and agreed to put it all in a letter. Your lawyer will no doubt talk to you about it when he visits next week to discuss your appeal.

The second piece of good news is that Harrison's old playgroup have confirmed that he was in attendance on the 21<sup>st</sup> July and there is nothing in their records to suggest he's ever had chickenpox. I also checked with your GP who confirmed there's nothing in his notes about chickenpox. Your lawyer has requested copies of the information from both and also asked for a statement from Jan about how she was denied access to Harrison, due to chickenpox, which he clearly didn't have. So, you were right. In both cases, we can prove she blatantly lied.

Although your lawyer's pleased about our findings, you mustn't get too excited just yet. He has warned that, unfortunately, we need more evidence for an appeal.

The third piece of good news is that I have secured a mortgage and put down a deposit on the three-bedroom house at Goldenbank. It should be ready next June.

Harrison and I had a great weekend, although of course, we were missing you loads. On Sunday we went to Dairyland, where Harrison insisted, he wanted a go on a pony ride. I was a bit worried, but he's a natural and so brave. He didn't even hold onto the saddle. We also bottle-fed the baby calves. I enclose photos. I know it's not the same as being with us, but I hope you still enjoy them.

It seems ages until the next visiting day. I think about you all the time and can't wait to see you again. Remember, I love you and have every faith that justice will eventually prevail. Keep strong and remember to eat.

Harrison sends you lots of love and kisses.

Love always, Ron XXXX

Beth scrubbed the steps with a hard bristle brush. Both hands together, she pushed and pulled, until soap bubbles spilled over onto the step below and soaked her knees. Tears ran down her cheeks. Bleddy Mad Mo, how could she have done this to her? And more to the point, why had she been allowed to get away with all those lies?

Her lawyer, Neil, had visited earlier that day. Although he was pleased with the information they'd discovered, and agreed it was proof that Maureen had been untruthful, it did not, he informed her, invalidate the evidence of the knife used by the judge to justify the custodial sentence. He'd also warned her that an appeal was unlikely to succeed if it was based solely on the fact that Maureen had told lies. After all, there was no way of getting around the fact that Beth herself had lied about seeing Jan that evening when, in fact, she was meeting Steve.

What was she going to do? The days appeared endless. How could she survive? Neil had tried to encourage her to think of the best scenario. She might win on appeal and be released immediately, or she could apply for parole halfway through her sentence. He'd tried to reassure her by explaining that the time she had spent in prison before the court case would count, so she could apply in two years and that, as long as she remained an exemplary prisoner, it was likely that she would be released at that stage. But it didn't help. It was still two years until then and by that time she would have missed so much of Harrison's childhood.

And how would Harrison take the news that his mother was a murderer and had spent time in prison? What would his school friends say? No, she couldn't face him. It was better that he thought she'd died. Ron would look after him. She trusted him to do that. It was better for them both if she was dead.

'Come on, Cinderella. You will go to the ball.'

Beth turned around. Jane stood on the bottom step, smiling.

'What?'

'You're needed in the office.'

Beth stood, dropped the brush in the bucket of soapy water and carried it down the stairs.

'You can leave those there for now. Follow me.'

Jane led her down the corridor until they arrived at a door with a glass viewing panel. Beth had been here before, on several occasions, including that morning to see Neil. Had he returned with more news?

'In you go, you have half an hour.'

Beth pushed open the door and stepped into the room.

'Mummy!'

She staggered back as a small tornado, otherwise known as Harrison, crashed into her belly. She reached down and swept him into her arms. Tears poured down her face as she hugged him tightly and kissed his cheek. She breathed in and drowned in the familiar smell of his hair shampoo and talcum powder. Glancing over her son's shoulder, she noticed Ron standing behind him, a huge grin on his face. She tried to swallow, but the lump in her throat and the taste of salt made her feel sick.

'Harrison, how did you get to be here? It's not even a visitin' day.'

'You have your favourite warder, Jane, to thank for this. She put a report into the Governor to say that your health was deteriorating and that, in her opinion, the only thing that could help would be a visit from Harrison. So here we are.'

'I've come to help you escape, Mummy.'

'What?' Beth lowered him slowly to the floor, sat on the chair and pulled him onto her knee.

'Like Paddington. He escaped in a balloon.'

Beth looked at Ron.

'It's okay, I've explained that you're in prison, but that it was like his favourite film; *Paddington 2*. You didn't do anything wrong, but the judge made a mistake and locked you up. I told him we're going to get you out, but of course, in the film, Paddington escapes to prove his innocence.'

'We're going to get you out, Mummy.'

'Not today, buddy. Remember I told you it might take a bit longer yet.' Ron ruffled Harrison's hair, leaned over and kissed the top of Beth's head.

'Mummy, you be home for Mismas?'

'I hope so, darlin'. I don't want to be away from you at Christmas, not when I've already missed your birthday. But we'll have to see.'

'I'm three now. I'm a big boy.'

Beth stroked his hair and kissed his forehead. 'I know you are, darlin'. You must have grown two inches since I saw you last.'

'I go to school now.'

'Do you like it?'

'Yes, I like counting, and dressing up, and the see-saw.' He climbed down from her knee and stood in front of her. 'I can do my letters. Look.' He began to sing to the tune of *Twinkle Twinkle Little Star*. 'A,B,C,D,E,F,G, - H,I K,K,L,M,N,O,P, - Q,R,S,T,U and V, - W,X,Y and Z. Now I know my A,B,C, next time come and sing with me.'

Ron laughed. 'Haven't quite got the J, K, bit right yet, but we're almost there.'

Beth clapped her hands. 'Oh, you're such a clever boy! Well done!' She pulled him back onto her knee and kissed his cheek again, and then again.

'Yuk, Mummy. You're making me wet.' He wiped his face with his sleeve.

'Sorry, darlin'. I'm just so pleased to see you.'

'And Daddy?'

'Yes, and Daddy.' Beth looked across at Ron. 'I'm guessin' the madwoman didn't approve?'

'Mummy, what you talking about?'

Ron reached over, lifted Harrison from Beth's knee and stood him in front of them, next to the coffee table. 'Adult stuff, buddy. Play with this sticker book for a while. I need to talk to Mummy for a minute.' Ron handed him a magazine and turned back to Beth. 'She's worried, as you would expect, but she's being very careful not to overstep the mark at the moment. What did your lawyer say about an appeal?'

'Not enough to go on as yet. We need to prove I didn't plan to take the knife to the scene – which is impossible. The only thing I can think is that my bag was on the coffee table. Maureen used the knife to open her envelope and somehow the knife finished up in my bag. But, as Neil pointed out, that's so unlikely. He said that the worse scenario is that I should get parole in two years, but at the moment that feels like a lifetime.' She watched Harrison as he struggled to take a sticker out of the magazine.

'Mummy do it?' He held the book up to her.

Beth peeled the sticker off of the page. 'Okay, darlin'. Here you go.' She passed the sticker to him, then turned back to face Ron. 'I can't face the thought of bein' away from him, even for another day. There must be more we can do?'

Ron took her hand in his and frowned. 'I wish I knew what. I feel so helpless.'

'I wonder...is it worth you talkin' to my neighbours? There's Audrey and Bill next door. He's Maureen's handyman, although they're also friends of hers so probably unlikely to offer any help. But then in my old house, there's Martin in Flat Two, Sue in Three and Vic in Four. I never got to know the new couple in my old flat, but you could check them out. See if anyone's noticed anythin' that could help us.'

'Mummy, you get this sticker for me?'

Beth bent the page slightly, pulled the corner of the sticker until it was free, and passed it to Harrison. 'Where should this one go?'

'Here.' Harrison placed the sticker carefully in the right place. The tip of his tongue stuck out from the corner of his mouth as he concentrated on getting the picture straight.

'Perfect. Well done.' Beth ruffled his hair.

Harrison giggled.

'Oh, Lordy me, I've missed that giggle. In fact, I've missed everythin' about you.'

'Don't cry, Mummy.'

Beth brushed away her tears and smiled at him. 'Better?'

Harrison nodded. 'Mummy, when you come home, can I have a puppy?'

'We'll see.'

'I'll look after it. I know how. We have a dog at school and we all brush him. His ears are all soft, similar to my toy rabbit.'

'*Similar,* that's a really good word. Well done. How is rabbit?'

'He's good.'

There was a knock on the door. Jane entered the room.

'Sorry folks, but time's up. Harrison, give your mummy a big kiss.'

Harrison threw his arms around Beth's neck and plonked a big kiss on her mouth.

'Do I get one of those?' Ron asked, and leaned towards her.

Beth kissed him, her lips tingled and her stomach flipped.

'Mm, I could get used to that.' Ron picked Harrison up. 'Come on, buddy. Time to go. Say bye-bye to Mummy.'

'Bye-bye, Mummy. See you later!'

'Let me know how he settles.'

'I'll write tomorrow, but don't worry, he'll be fine.'

Jane followed Ron to the door. 'Stay here 'til I return, Beth. I have to take these two to the end of the corridor and then I'll be back for you.'

Beth's heart sank as the door closed behind them. This was unbearable. Unbearable if she didn't see them and unbearable if she did. Her chest ached. She simply had to show them that she hadn't planned to kill Steve, that she hadn't put that knife in her handbag deliberately. Why would she? All she had to do was prove it.

But how?

# Chapter Nineteen

Maureen breathed in deeply to enjoy the comforting smell of banana cake batter. She'd hoped baking would take her mind off the dread she experienced when Ron announced he was taking Harrison to see Beth. She'd tried so hard to persuade Ron that it wasn't a good idea, but he wouldn't listen. She looked at the kitchen clock. They'd be there with her soon.

She greased the bread tin with butter, poured in the batter and put it on the centre shelf of the hot oven. Everyone enjoyed her banana cake. It had been Giles's favourite. She'd been cooking one for him on the day she discovered his dreadful betrayal. Why did he have to ruin everything?

The cake was in the oven, when she realised that she was short of a cake tin. Her usual one was still full of breakfast muffins. She explored the pantry but found nothing suitable. Perhaps it would be okay wrapped in tin foil? Reaching for the box, she pulled the edge and sighed with frustration as a five-inch remnant of foil came loose in her hand. Had she got time to nip to the corner shop? No, the doctor was due for his weekly visit anytime soon.

Then she remembered the day Giles had finished working at the office to go on sick leave, three months before. He'd come home with a large tin of Quality

Street and she'd teased him about developing a sweet tooth. He'd explained that it was an empty tin he found at the office, left over from Christmas, and how he'd used it to carry home the small items from his desk drawers. It had been in the hall cupboard ever since.

She collected a large freezer bag from the pantry, carried the sweet tin into the lounge and began to transfer Giles's items into the bag. She smiled at his pencil sharpener shaped like the Eiffel Tower that someone had obviously brought back from their holiday. A pen and pencil set that she'd given to him for a birthday present came next. She transferred a mouse mat with squidgy oily bubbles – like a sixty's lava lamp – and a ruler they'd bought together when they'd visited the Eden Project.

A small photograph fell to the floor. It must have been stuck to the underside of the mouse mat. She felt a warm flush of affection as she picked it up. She didn't have Giles down as a sentimentalist, keeping pictures of her or Anna in his desk like that. She turned it over and gasped at the image, not of her or Anna, but of a young woman with long wavy red hair, amazing eyes, thick black eyelashes and perfectly groomed eyebrows. Maureen never bothered to shape her own eyebrows, but always admired how good they looked on other women when they were done well. The woman's rosebud lips, smiled at whoever was taking the photograph, warm and affectionate. Who was she?

She waited until the doctor had gone, and then took a tray of tea and a slice of banana cake up to Giles, put it on the side-table and poured him a cup. She pressed the bed control button to raise him into a sitting position and sat in the chair beside him.

'You're so good to me.' He smiled. 'I don't deserve you.'

'Nonsense, we all get what we deserve. I'm a firm believer in karma.'

'Is that banana bread you've been baking? It smells wonderful.'

'I hadn't got a cake tin spare so I had to raid your old Quality Street tin from your office, I'm afraid. Hope you don't mind.'

'Why would I? I haven't touched it since the day I left. I'm glad it came in useful. What's mine is yours, you've always known that. We vowed as much on the day of our marriage, do you remember that?'

'I remember we promised to be true to each other in good times and in bad, in sickness and in health, and to love and honour each other for all the days of our lives.'

Giles reached over and took Maureen's hand in his. 'I'm so sorry you drew the short straw. I can't believe you've had to nurse me like this. This damn cancer, it's not fair on you.'

Maureen reached into her pocket, took out the photograph and put it on the table beside Giles's tea. 'Life can be very unfair. Do you want to explain this?'

Giles picked up the photograph. His complexion was already pale, but what little colour he had left drained from his face. 'Where-'

'It was in the tin.'

She glared at him as tears filled his eyes.

'It's difficult to explain.'

'Well you'd better start now, or I'll be ringing the hospice to book you in. And I'll make sure you never see Anna again.'

The tears trickled down his cheeks and dripped onto the bedclothes. He sniffed. 'I was working three days a week in London at the time. We were expecting Anna, and you were...understandably...reluctant to make love.'

'Don't make this out to be my fault.'

'I wasn't trying to...honestly. We met at the London office, when she came to work as a temp. She was beautiful, kind and somehow...it just happened. It only lasted for about three months. I came to my senses as soon as Anna was born. I didn't know I still had the photograph. I'm sorry.'

'Sorry you were caught out?'

'I was just saying...I ended it and I've never been unfaithful ever again. Please, Maureen, I chose you. Please forgive me.'

The rage that built inside her, felt like a pressure cooker about to explode in her head. 'How could you?' She raised her arm and slapped him hard across the face. 'How could you? Answer me!' Her voice rose to a shrill scream. She watched as the bright red handprint brought colour back to his face.

Giles lifted his hand and stroked his cheek. He looked down at his cup of tea. 'I deserved that,' he mumbled.

'Karma. Your sins have found you out. I hope you die a painful death.' She grabbed the picture, tore it into tiny pieces and threw them at him. 'Don't expect any lunch. I'm going for a walk to clear my head.'

She turned on her heals and stormed out of the room.

Reaching the hall, she grabbed her coat, slipped on her shoes and left by the front door, slamming it behind her. She walked down to the Gylly Café, ordered a coffee and found a seat as far away from the loud speaker as she could. Music was okay, but only when it didn't hurt your eardrums and at least here she had a good window seat with a fantastic view out to sea.

She jumped as the waitress appeared at her shoulder holding Maureen's order. The waitress smiled as she put it in front of Maureen, then twisted the saucer around so that the frothy heart on top of the coffee was perfectly positioned.

'Enjoy the rest of your day.'

Enjoy the rest of her day? That would never happen ever again. How could it after this? She had never, ever considered the fact that Giles would be unfaithful to her. How could he? They'd been so close, devoted even. These past few months she'd looked after him, showered him with care, love and affection – quite literally in sickness and in health. That would end today. There had to be ways to pay him back for this, hurt him in any way she could for the remainder of the time they had left together. She stirred her coffee vigorously. The teaspoon had clinked against the cup and the froth had sploshed into the saucer as she'd sworn under her breath that she'd make him pay.

And she had.

She sniffed and glanced at the clock: an hour and a quarter since she'd put the cake in. It would be ready now. She grabbed her oven gloves and opened the oven door. Mm, it smelt delicious. The trick was to allow it to cool down before taking that first slice. She'd never managed it yet.

Ron and Harrison would be on their way back now. Harrison loved her banana cake. Ron would no doubt give in to Harrison's demands for a McDonald's before they got back, but hopefully he'd still find space for a slice.

Beth opened Ron's letter. Maureen had been convinced that a prison visit would damage Harrison. Hopefully he was far more resilient than Maureen gave him credit. She unfolded the letter and read:

Dear Beth,

It was so hard to leave you yesterday. I was gutted. Fortunately, Harrison kept my spirits up while we drove back. He hardly stopped talking about you, apart from a bit of a sing-along and this version of his favourite song:

> *Twinkle, twinkle chocolate bar*
> *My daddy drives a rusty car*
> *Push the lever, pull the choke*
> *Off we go with lots of smoke.*
> *Twinkle, twinkle chocolate bar*
> *My daddy drives a rusty car.*

Actually, my car's not that bad, old maybe, but it's not rusty. As you know, Maureen's usually very possessive about bedtimes – her domain – but Harrison was understandably a bit clingy when I was about to leave and she asked if I wanted to take him up to bed. As we finished his bed-time story, he threw his arms around my neck, begged me not to go and started to cry. He said that he woke up at night and *'was lonely.'* I told him he only had to shout for Nana Mo. He got quite upset with me, reckoned that he did shout and shout, but no one came. I asked when this happened and he said it was *'yesterday,'* but then, as you know, anything that's not happened today, happened yesterday, whether it was a week past, two days ago, or sometime in his earliest memories. I cuddled him and, I think, reassured him. Told him it was either a bad dream, or possibly that Maureen was in the shower.

I thought I'd better mention it to Maureen, expecting her to simply laugh it off, but instead she got angry. She insisted that she always has the monitor on all night and even takes it with her when she has a shower. Eventually I managed to calm her down. I should have been in the Diplomatic Service, rather than the Navy.

Anyway, he was fast asleep before I left and I'm sure he'll be fine. I'm picking him up from nursery school tonight. It's my early night and I've promised him we'll visit the new exhibition at the Maritime Museum – *creatures from the deep* – followed by a pizza. I can't wait until I see you next time and I will treasure that goodbye kiss until then.

Love you forever, Ron, XXXX

Thank goodness, Dearovim. Harrison had bounced back from the visit without too many obvious issues. More upset about Maureen not hearing him shout when she was in the shower than he was about her being in prison. Perhaps she would be able to see him again. Even if it was only every so often it would be better than not seeing him at all.

# Chapter Twenty

Dear Beth,

I've made some progress, well of sorts. Following your suggestion, I visited the neighbours. I was losing heart after speaking to most of them, but then, just as I was about to leave, Vic suddenly remembered something. Apparently, she was going to work on the morning of your arrest when she saw the police car draw up in front of Maureen's gate. At the time, she only thought about the police car and wondered what was going on. It was sometime later that she realised it had pulled into the space where Maureen always parks. As she uses the Morris so infrequently, it hardly ever moves from its normal spot. When Vic got home later that day, the Morris was parked back in its usual space. It may be nothing, but it's a puzzle.

I spent the weekend at a football camp with Harrison. He looks great in his Plymouth Argyle kit. It was really good fun. Twenty-two boys (and their dads) playing football, camping and cooking over campfires. Not only did they teach the boys ball control, but they also taught them how to stay safe. The campsite was a little way from the football ground, so we practised crossing the road. That was quite straightforward for Harrison because he already has good road sense. Then we played Stranger Danger. The dads had to pretend to be walking along with their son, just a casual walk until the coach blew his whistle and shouted *'Stranger Danger.'* Then we dads had to morph into being child snatchers. The boys had to kick their dads – now villains – on the shins, pull their hand free and run to safety – a groundsheet in the middle of the playing field. Harrison was really good at it, as my bruises prove, even though I was wearing shin pads. They also taught the boys to cook sausages and marshmallows safely over the campfire.

We both miss you so much. I've managed to get a day off to visit you the first week of November, so send me a visitor form. I can't wait to see you. In the meantime, let me know if you think of any more lines of enquiry.

All my love, Ron, XXXXX

Maureen watched Audrey struggle down the steps, closed the front door and returned to the kitchen.

How dare he. How *could* Ron go around asking her friends and neighbours if they'd seen anything suspicious on the night of the murder? Beth had put him up to this, Maureen was sure of it.

Audrey had said she'd given Ron short shift, but what about the other neighbours? What did Ron hope to achieve by nosing around like this? It was an absolute betrayal, especially after all she'd done for Harrison.

Yet another unjust betrayal in a line of many. First Giles, then Anna and now this. She'd never forgiven

Giles and it had taken over a year and that special announcement before she allowed Anna back into her life.

She picked up the coffee cups, and shoved them into the sink, then twisted the tap hard. Water gushed against the bowl and splashed over the front of her blouse. She leant forward, gripping the edge of the unit.

Three weeks, three long empty weeks, had passed since Harrison's visit. He'd filled Beth with hope at the thought that she'd surely be back with him soon? But her initial excitement had quickly deflated like a punctured balloon. There was little progress.

The key turned in the lock and Jane poked her head around the door. 'Ready for that good-looking husband of yours?'

'I suppose.'

'I suppose? Come on, surely you can show a little more enthusiasm? I'd be excited by the thought of a hunk like that waiting to see me.'

'Not if you were stuck in here, you wouldn't.'

'Point taken.' Jane stood back from the doorway allowing Beth to walk in front of her.

Beth trudged down the familiar corridor that led to the visiting room. She was excited to be seeing Ron again, of course she was. She could still remember the taste of him as he tenderly kissed her goodbye last month. Her lips had tingled for days. But seeing him and hearing news of Harrison, only made her loneliness worse the next day. It was like being on a rollercoaster, up one minute and down the next. A glint of hope with the proof of Maureen's lies, followed by despair when they realised it wasn't enough for an appeal. Beth forced a smile as she walked across to join Ron.

He reached over and kissed her cheek. 'How's it going?' he asked, as they both sat down.

'Okay, I suppose. I just miss Harrison all the time. Tell me what you've been up to.'

Beth sat and listened, while Ron told her about their visits to the beach, a trip to the seal sanctuary and the new bike he'd bought for Harrison, with little stabiliser wheels.

'We go for trips around the lake at Swanpool.' Ron reached for her hand. 'What's up? You don't seem yourself today.'

'I've decided we need a new approach. It's no use tryin' to solve this bleddy knife business.' Beth leaned forward and whispered. 'I've been thinkin'…I know this is a big leap…but what if I didn't do it?'

'What?'

'What if someone else stabbed Steve?'

'You're joking?

'I know, it's crazy, but think about it. I can't remember anythin' after Steve arrived in Falmouth at about eight-thirty, or just after. I must have passed out then, otherwise surely, I would have remembered bits of the journey or arrivin' at his place. But I don't. Nothing. Not after I shouted at him for bein' late. I don't even know how I got into his car.'

'But the doctor agreed…loss of memory is part of Pathological Intoxication.'

'I know, and I've done things before that I can't remember, such as when I wrecked Mum's pottery collection, but only when I was on the edge of unconsciousness, not after I'd already blacked out.'

Ron ran his fingers through his hair. 'I can't get my head around this. You're saying you might be completely innocent after all?'

'Look, the pathologist said Steve had been stabbed between nine o'clock and ten. You know I've never woken up so quickly before. That would mean I woke after only an hour or so, and then passed out again for another seven. That doesn't sound right, does it?'

'Now you come to mention it, you're right. Once you blackout, you're usually out cold until the next morning.'

'So, it doesn't make sense, then, does it?'

Ron stared at her. 'Oh my God, Beth.'

'Look, could you ask around in Helston? See if anyone noticed anythin'. Anythin' at all.'

'Like what?'

'I don't know. Perhaps see if you can speak to his workmates at Greggs. Ask them if he'd fallen out with anyone lately? Did he have any enemies? Or...anythin' like that.'

Ron shook his head. 'I'll do what I can, but I imagine the police have been all over this.'

Beth shook her head. 'No, that's the point. They already thought they had the killer. Me. Even I didn't really question whether I actually did it or not, just whether I meant to. But if I didn't do it, someone else must have.' Beth reached over and grabbed Ron's hand. 'Come on, Ron. You can do this.'

'I'll do my utmost. You know I will.' Ron lifted her hand and kissed her knuckles.

Jane shouted across the room. 'Five minutes, folks! Start to wrap it up, please!'

Beth glanced across to Jane. 'I'm sure her watch is fast.' She turned back to Ron. 'I was also wonderin'… would it be worth it for us to put up a poster on Steve's street, somewhere near his place, and appeal for any information about the night of the murder?'

'I could offer a reward. It'll have to be quite small – all my savings have gone on the house deposit – but I could offer a hundred.'

'Worth a try.' Beth smiled. 'Thanks, Ron. I appreciate what you're doin' for me. Really, I do.'

I do. The words echoed in her mind bringing a fleeting memory of their wedding almost four years before. For better, for worse. So far, apart from the birth of Harrison, they had mostly endured the worse and, on reflection she realised, that was almost entirely her fault. But instead of walking away, Ron was here supporting her and working hard to live up to his promises.

She squeezed his hand. 'You'd better go. Jane will take off if she flaps her arms anymore.'

'I love you, Beth. I won't let you down.'

'I know.' She leaned across the table and kissed him full on the lips.

His eyes brimmed with tears as he pulled her to her feet. 'Bye, darling. See you soon.'

'Love you,' she called out as he got to the door.

Oops, she hadn't meant to say that, but what the heck. She'd suddenly realised that she did, and always had. She'd built a wall of defence around her and Harrison, locked away her emotions, but then, over the past few weeks, those barriers had completely melted away. She had to find a way back to him and Harrison. And to do that, they had to find out who had really killed Steve.

# Chapter Twenty-one

Maureen sat in her armchair. She reached over and picked up her latest book, desperate for a distraction. These days, Harrison and Ron were out every weekend and most evenings. She had far too much time on her hands.

She opened the book. It was an old edition of a Dickens novel. It smelled quite musty. Five minutes later, she put it down. This was hopeless; she couldn't concentrate. Scary thoughts wriggled into her mind and refused to leave her alone.

That night back in May had begun just as she'd planned. She knew that Beth became argumentative and violent after a couple of glasses of wine. Both Steve and Beth's mother had said as much. While Beth was reading through the legal documents, Maureen had ensured that Beth's glass was constantly topped up, while keeping her own drinking to an absolute minimum.

When Beth left the house, by the back door, Maureen had grabbed her coat, slipped on her shoes, picked up her house keys and followed. She walked quickly to the back gate, opened it slightly and peered around. Beth stood on the other side of Melville Road, glancing at her watch, frowning and tapping her foot.

This was looking good. Steve was late and Beth was not too happy about it. Maureen kept the back gate cracked open, just enough for her to continue watching.

Ten minutes went by before a car pulled up. Steve clambered out of the driver's seat, walked round to the passenger door and opened it wide. He tried to embrace Beth but she pushed him away.

'Where the hell 'av you been?'

'Sorry. The traffic into Falmouth's really bad. Must be a do on in town.'

'I felt like a bleddy prostitute stood here.'

'You don't look like one.' Steve grinned, put his arm on her shoulder and tried to pull her closer. 'You look great.'

Beth stepped back, stumbled and fell, landing on her backside. 'Now look what you've made me do!'

'Sorry.' He reached out his hand.

Beth pushed it away. 'Don't touch me.'

Maureen smiled. This was working even better than she'd planned. As she continued to watch, Beth staggered to her feet and swayed, but then she appeared to collapse into Steve's arms.

'Beth, what's the matter? Have you been drinking? Oh Shit, wake up, Beth!'

Maureen's stomach lurched. How could Beth be passing out already? It was too soon. She was supposed to have an ugly row with Steve and stomp back to spend the rest of the evening at home. The argument had hardly begun. She watched as Steve lowered Beth carefully into the car and fastened the seat belt over her. He closed her door, walked around to the driver's side and got in. As the car pulled away, Maureen realised that Beth's handbag was still lying on the pavement. She nipped through the gateway, crossed the road and picked it up.

Re-entering the kitchen, she pondered her next move. She had to do more. She needed to keep Beth and Steve apart, to stop any chance of them moving in together and taking Harrison with them. Harrison had to stay here with her, whatever it took. 'Think Maureen. What to do?'

The front doorbell rang.

Maureen looked across the hall towards the door. She could see Steve's outline through the stained-glass door panel. He rang the bell again. What was he doing? He'd wake Harrison. She could stop him making such a racket by opening the door, but if she did that and he brought Beth back now, tonight would become Maureen's Groundhog Day. Beth wouldn't remember any of tonight and she'd forgive Steve everything. But even worse, how would Beth react when she realised Maureen knew she'd lied and was meeting Steve, not Jan? There would be no going back from that level of deceit; she'd leave and take Harrison with her.

Maureen picked up the steak knife, clutched it tightly in her hand and tip-toed into the hall. The light was off, so she was sure Steve couldn't see her. Perhaps he'd use Beth's keys and open the door. She could stab him – she'd stabbed someone before. She could always say she thought he was an intruder. She would be seen as a hero, defending herself and Harrison against a violent criminal. How was she to know it was a case of mistaken identity until after it was too late and Steve lay dead? Steve and Beth wouldn't be able to get back together again if he was dead.

Maureen clutched the knife a little tighter and edged forward.

Steve turned and disappeared down the steps. Beth's keys must be in her handbag. He wouldn't be able to get in after all.

Maureen ran to the front door, cracked it open and watched as Steve returned to the car and got in. She could see him fussing over Beth, making sure the seatbelt wasn't rubbing on her neck. Why was he being so thoughtful? He was the villain in this whole sorry saga; trying to tempt Beth away, encouraging her to tell lies, making Beth deceitful. He was a bad influence and should not be allowed to become a part of Harrison's life.

Steve's car started to move. They were getting away. She had to do something.

Maureen shoved the knife into Beth's handbag, grabbed her car keys from the dish on the windowsill and stepped outside. As Steve negotiated a three-point turn and pulled away, Maureen shut the door behind her and rushed down the steps. She jumped into Giles's Morris. The engine started first time. It took several attempts to turn the car around – more like a nine-point turn, rather than three – but eventually she was heading onto Melville Road in pursuit.

Which way? She had to catch them up before they made the Helston turnoff or she'd never find Steve's place. Heart racing, she sped past McDonalds and Sainsbury's, then turned left up the hill towards the bypass, hoping against hope that this was the route they would have taken. As she sped past Asda, she thought she saw Steve's vehicle three cars in front. At the roundabout she had to wait for two cars coming from her right. Panicking, she turned onto the Helston road and put her foot down. That had to be them, surely?

'Oh, my God, hurry up!' she shouted at the car in front. At this rate she'd never catch up with them. She flicked on her indicator and pulled out to overtake. She couldn't remember ever being so brave before, but as she pressed her foot to the floor and her vehicle zoomed past the offending slowcoach, she experienced a surge of adrenalin. She was enjoying this.

A blue car appeared in front of her but it wasn't Steve's. Again, she indicated and pulled out to overtake, but this time a car was coming towards her with flashing headlights. She pulled in, narrowly missing the bonnet of the blue car. Both drivers blasted their horns in protest, but she didn't care. Harrison was worth the risk. *Oh, my God...Harrison!* What if he woke up and found himself alone? She forced herself to concentrate on her driving; she couldn't worry about Harrison just now. After all, he hardly ever woke at night. She breathed deeply, willing herself to stay calm.

Racing through the next village, her eyes were momentarily distracted by a flash of light in her rear-view mirror but then, suddenly, not far in front, she saw Steve's car. She slowed to maintain her distance.

Steve drove onto the outskirts of Helston, turned right at the roundabout and then turned again, this time into a narrow residential road. Maureen followed. Steve parked his car half way down the road. Maureen spotted a space and pulled in three cars behind him. Slumped down in her seat, she peeped over the dashboard and watched as he clambered out and walked around to open the passenger door.

'Are you okay there, Steve?'

'Oh, hi, Derek. It's my bird, Beth. She's not feeling well. Could you give me a hand getting her indoors?'

The two men manoeuvred Beth out of the car. They propped her up between them, draped her arms over their shoulders and dragged her into the house. After a couple of minutes, they reappeared on the front doorstep.

'Thanks, Derek. See you when you get back from your spell out on the rigs. I owe you a drink.'

'Won't be for three months, but I'll hold you to that.' Derek waved at him and then walked towards Maureen's car. He glanced towards her as he walked past and then turned into the next gateway, unlocked the front door and disappeared into the house.

Maureen considered her options. She could go home to Falmouth and await Beth's return, and then be constantly tormented by the fear that Beth and Steve would eventually get together and move Harrison away from her. It might not even be Steve who tempted her away; Beth could meet someone else with the same result – Maureen would lose Harrison. That wasn't going to happen. Her only real option was to do something about it. She'd come too far to go back now.

She picked up Beth's bag, clambered out and approached Steve's front door. Her heart pounded as she rang the doorbell.

'Maureen. What are you doing here?'

'I've brought Beth's bag. She dropped it in the street.'

'What's happening with Harrison? Who's looking after him?'

'My neighbour.'

'You'd better come in.' Steve opened the door wider and stood aside. 'Go through into the kitchen. It's that door at the end of the hall.'

Maureen entered the kitchen. A large round wall clock with Roman numerals drew her attention. It ticked loudly; tick-tock, tick-tock. Goodness 9:15 p.m., time was passing. She needed to hurry things along and get back to Harrison. She put Beth's bag on the table and turned to face Steve.

He frowned. 'I don't understand why you've come all this way, just to deliver Beth's bag.'

'She'll need her keys.'

'That's nonsense, she could just ring your bell. Although, thinking about it, I just tried that. Where were you?'

Maureen's voice stuck in her throat.

'How did you know where to find me?' Steve towered over her. 'Did you follow us?'

She shook her head. She wanted to turn and run but her legs shook so much she couldn't move. In any case, if she gave up now things would be even worse. Beth would no doubt decide that she was unstable and incapable of looking after Harrison. Of course, she wasn't really unbalanced, just desperate.

'I don't believe you, Maureen. You must have followed us. Harrison's on his own, isn't he? How could you? I'm ringing the police.' He turned his back on her and picked up his mobile.

Maureen delved into Beth's bag and grabbed the steak knife. 'I wouldn't do that if I were you.'

'It's the quickest way to get someone to him and make sure he's safe.' Steve turned back to face her. His eyes widened. 'Maureen, put that knife down. You'll hurt yourself.'

'That's what Tony said. He deserved to die, and so do you.' Maureen threw herself forward and thrust the knife into Steve's chest. This time she made sure she plunged it in as hard as she could. Steve's legs crumpled, he sank to the floor and collapsed, falling onto his side. He could have been asleep if it wasn't for the blood that spread across his chest and dribbled onto the tiles beside him.

Maureen's heart was racing. The familiar metallic smell of blood made her gag. She felt Steve's neck for a pulse. Nothing.

She wanted to run, but she knew she had more to do if she was going to ensure her relationship with Harrison remained as it was. Steve's death may have solved one problem, but now she had to make sure Beth didn't cause any more. Taking care to avoid the puddle of blood, she leaned over and tugged the knife from Steve's chest. Using a handkerchief from her pocket, she wiped the handle clean.

Returning to the hall, she pushed open the first door with her foot, and the smell of bleach and shower gel wafted over her. The bathroom was tiled dark green and furnished with an old-fashioned WC and rolled top bath, which Maureen thought would have been quite nice, had they been clean. Dirty, damp towels lay on the floor. Maureen sniffed. She had been right: this was no place for Harrison. She turned away and pushed her elbow against the next door, which swung open to reveal the bedroom.

Maureen could see Beth laid out on the bed, dead to the world. She moved to Beth's side and stood looking down at her. Déjà vu, except unlike when she'd discovered Anna, she could see Beth was breathing steadily. But what should she do about Beth? After all, she couldn't back down now. Should she stab Beth as she slept, and hope the police believed this was a double murder? Or could she make it look like Beth had committed the murder and then taken her own life? Maureen shook her head. Not very likely, and anyway, she had fond memories of their times together with Harrison. Beth was a good mother and, in some ways, she reminded Maureen of Anna. No, Beth didn't need to die, but she could take the blame.

Maureen put the knife in Beth's hand, pressing her fingers onto the handle.

Using the handkerchief and taking care not to smudge Beth's fingerprints, she returned to the kitchen. She placed the knife carefully on the floor beside Steve and stuffed the bloody handkerchief back into her pocket. Using a fresh handkerchief, she closed the front door behind her and scurried back to Giles's Morris.

The drive home was a blur, like being on autopilot. Maureen did, however, remember stopping in Falmouth and shoving the bloody handkerchief into a road-side rubbish bin. Arriving home, she was annoyed to discover that someone had taken her normal space, forcing her to park further up the road. How dare they.

She shrugged off her coat and raced up the stairs to Harrison's room. For the first time that evening, an icy strand of fear pierced her chest. What if he had woken and she hadn't been there for him? What if something had happened to him? She hardly dared look.

Harrison lay on his back, one arm over his head and the other clutching his fluffy blue rabbit. Sleeping peacefully. It didn't look as though he'd moved at all. Her heart swelled with pride. He looked like an angel and now he was hers. Steve was dead and Beth would be blamed.

Maureen's book slipped from the arm of her chair and landed on the floor with a thump. She opened her eyes and blinked, then pushed herself up out of her chair, walked into the kitchen and switched on the kettle. Her heart was beating far too fast. No one would ever suspect her involvement in Steve's death, so why couldn't she shake off this overwhelming sense of dread?

# Chapter Twenty-two

Beth ripped open the letter, shredding the envelope in her haste. Her heart raced as the adrenalin surged through her. Please, please let him have found a way to get her home.

Dear Beth,

I called in at Gregg's this week-end, no joy I'm afraid. I didn't let on why I was asking about Steve, just asked if this was the place where that guy worked who was murdered back in May. Everyone I spoke to in the shop said he was a really nice guy. Everyone liked him. No enemies. However, the good news is that I received a phone call from a guy called Derek, a mate of Steve's and also a neighbour. He saw our poster asking for information and invited me to join him for a drink at the pub. He says he may have some information for me, but unfortunately, he wasn't prepared to go into any detail over the phone. I've asked your lawyer, Neil, to join me for two reasons:

a) It may give us a lead.
b) I don't want to walk in on an ambush of vigilantes.

I've got to dash now. I have to get this in the post so that you get it tomorrow morning in time to book a phone call. Ring me tomorrow night, if possible after Harrison's bedtime – say about eight – and I'll give you an update.

All my love, Ron XXXX

The warder – a new one who hadn't even bothered to introduce herself – walked Beth to the phone and presented her with a phone card.

'Here you go. Make the most of it. You were lucky to get one at such short notice.'

Beth took the card, and with her hands trembling, slid it into the machine and tapped in Ron's mobile number.

He answered immediately. 'Beth, I've got great news.'

Her heart skipped a beat. 'Tell me, quickly.'

'Neil and I met with Derek. He confirmed that he helped Steve carry you out of the car and take you through to the bedroom. He said Steve had told him you always passed out like that after a couple of drinks and you'd be completely out of it until the morning.'

'Why didn't he tell the police before?'

'Apparently, he went away in the early hours of the next morning and missed all the police house-to-house enquiries. He works on the rigs and has only recently got back. It was all over and done with by the time he came home. He'd heard about Steve's death, but not the details, so he never linked the night he helped Steve carry you in and the date of the murder. Not until he saw our poster.'

Beth could feel the tears burning the back of her eyes. 'Ron...'

'Don't cry darling. Neil, says this is really good news. He contacted your medical specialist, who confirmed that considering the state Derek said you were in, it's unlikely you would have regained consciousness. So, his evidence proves you were unconscious at the time of the murder. Neil has made an appointment first thing with your barrister and the judge because your imprisonment is likely to be a miscarriage of justice.'

'What does that mean?'

'It means you could be out of prison by lunchtime tomorrow, and you could be home in time to put Harrison to bed.'

Beth's head spun. She grabbed a nearby chair and collapsed onto it.

'Are you alright?' The warder moved towards her.

'I'm fine.' Beth waved her away. 'Ron, does this mean I'll be free?'

'From what I can gather, you'll be released on parole while the police re-open the case and make further enquiries. We're not home and dry just yet, but we're certainly on our way.'

'Oh, Ron.' Beth brushed the tears from her cheeks. 'What if it all goes wrong?'

'Don't worry, Neil's convinced. He'll get a message to you as soon as we've seen the judge. And if they're going to let you out tomorrow, I'll come down and pick you up.'

Beth walked back to her cell in a daze. Tomorrow, she could be reunited with Harrison. And Ron. She could hardly believe it. But suppose something went wrong? Neil could be mistaken. He'd been convinced she'd get off with a non-custodial sentence, only to be proved wrong. Please let him be right this time. Please let it be true.

She entered her cell and hardly noticed as the door clanged behind her and the key turned in the lock. Picking up the photograph of Harrison holding his birthday cake, she smiled and kissed the picture. Tomorrow, buddy, tomorrow, I'll be there to kiss you goodnight. She lay on the bed and allowed her thoughts to drift towards tomorrow and her first hug with Harrison.

Half an hour later she sat up. Her head felt as though a hammer was battering her brain. She needed to think things through. She was missing something, but what? Every time something began to float into her consciousness it just as quickly disappeared. She held her head in her hands and cried out with the pain. Sod's Law – she was probably about to be released tomorrow and now she was dying with a stroke or a brain tumour.

She reached behind her and pushed the alarm bell. A couple of minutes later, the cell door opened and Jane entered. Clare stood in the doorway behind her.

'Beth, whatever's the matter. You look dreadful.' Jane rushed to Beth's side.

'I'm dyin'.' Beth sobbed. 'I've got a thunderin' head, feel sick and the lights are flickerin'. I'm going to die, just when they might let me go home.'

'Nonsense, you've got a migraine.'

'I don't get migraines.'

'Welcome to my world. I can tell you everything there is to know about 'em.' Jane spoke into her radio. 'Come on, Beth. We'll take you to sickbay. You need some painkillers and sleeping tablets. You'll be fine in the morning.'

Beth held onto Jane's arm as she and Clare escorted Beth to the infirmary.

Jane helped her get into bed, tucked her in and waited while the doctor administered tablets. 'I'll leave you in good hands, Beth. You can have a lie-in tomorrow, breakfast in bed and then I'll be over to check on you. Sweet dreams.'

'Thanks,' Beth mumbled, as she drifted off to sleep.

# Chapter Twenty-three

Maureen held out Harrison's coat. 'Come on, Harrison, let's get you ready. We need to go to the shops.'

'Can I have some Milky Stars?'

'Can I have some Milky Stars, what?'

'Please, Nana Mo.'

'If you're a good boy. No, that's the wrong arm, silly.'

Harrison giggled and turned around to put the right arm into his coat sleeve.

'Now the other one. Oh, blast, that's the phone. Try and get your coat on yourself while I get that.' Maureen dashed to the phone table in the hall and picked up the receiver.

'Hello, is that Mrs James of thirty-two Emilia Boulevard?'

'Speaking.' Maureen didn't recognise the voice. Was this another of those scammers?

'This is Lucinda Terry, duty officer at Exmouth Women's Prison. Can you please confirm for me...will this be Beth Taylor's address after she leaves here on parole today?'

'What?'

'Mrs Taylor is being released today and I need to confirm her place of residence.'

Maureen sank onto the settle. How could this possibly be? She'd thought her life with Harrison was safe for months yet. Surely there hadn't been time for an appeal? She would have heard about it.

'No one told me she was being let out. What's this all about?'

'I'm afraid I can't discuss that with you. I'm sure she'll be able to tell you herself before the end of the day, but I need to verify this will be her address.'

Maureen hesitated. If she refused to take Beth back, that would presumably mean Beth was homeless. But then Social Services would get involved and Harrison would be taken away. That couldn't happen, she wouldn't let him go.

It was clearly time to implement Plan B.

She confirmed that Beth would be living back at Emilia Boulevard and hurriedly replaced the receiver.

'Harrison? We have to go out. Sit in the lounge and don't move while I sort things out.'

Maureen dashed upstairs, threw her clothes into one suitcase, Harrison's things into another, and dragged them both downstairs. She grabbed her shopping bag and filled it with food from the pantry. A second bag was filled with boots, shoes and slippers from the settle. Then she collected the remaining money from the shoebox in her bureau and shoved it into her large shoulder bag.

'Come on, Harrison. We're going on an adventure. Bring rabbit and blanket.'

'Where we going, Nana Mo?'

'On holiday. Come on, quickly now.' Maureen picked up her car keys and opened the front door. She grabbed the handle of one suitcase with one hand and Harrison's hand in the other. The suitcase clattered down the steps behind her as they descended. Maureen hoped the wheels would at least make it to the car.

She strapped Harrison into his car seat, struggling to work out how the clasp worked as she had only used it once before. Eventually, it clipped into place and she raced back up the steps to retrieve the second suitcase and the two bags, pulling the front door shut behind her.

She opened the rear doors of the Morris and lifted the suitcases and bags inside.

'Off we go, Harrison.'

She sighed with relief as the car started, despite the fact that she hadn't used it for months. Thank goodness Giles chose such a reliable car. But then, he always had good taste; he chose her, didn't he?

# Chapter Twenty-four

Jane handed Beth a carrier bag. 'These are all the items Godzilla confiscated from you on admission day. Sign here if everything is present and correct.'

'Isn't she here today?'

'I asked if I could do your discharge, Beth. I wanted to wish you all the best for the future.'

Beth gave her a hug. 'You've been a good friend, Jane. Thanks. And thanks for lookin' after me last night. I really thought I was dyin'.'

Jayne touched Beth's shoulder and lowered her voice. 'I've seen enough villains in my time, Beth, and as far as I'm concerned, you're not one of them. Perhaps you didn't put that knife in your bag? So, think about it... who could have?'

'The only other person there was Maureen.'

'Exactly. The same person who stitched you up in court and continued to enjoy life out there with your son, while you were stuck in here.' Jane pushed the door wide open. 'Now, get out there and prove your innocence.'

Jane walked with Beth, guiding her out of the office and down to the gate. Beth could see Ron waiting for her on the other side of the fence, a huge smile on his face. The grass had been cut that morning, probably for the last time that year. It smelt wonderful. A guard unlocked the gate and opened it wide.

Beth paused and hugged Jane again. 'Thanks for everything. I'll write and let you know how things go.' She rushed through the gate and fell into Ron's arms. He hugged her tightly.

Beth grabbed his hand. 'Come on. Let's get out of here before they change their minds.'

The gravel crunched beneath the car's tyres as they pulled off the car park and onto the tarmac drive. They had to stop at a pair of high-security gates and show Beth's release papers before the gates were opened, but then they were able to pull out onto the main road.

'How long will it take us to get back?' Beth asked.

'About two hours, although I need to stop for petrol the first chance we get. I'm practically running on fumes. Didn't want to stop on the way and be late getting here.'

They found a petrol station about half a mile down the road. Ron filled the car and returned with two boxes of sandwiches, two packets of crisps and two bottles of water. 'Meal Deal. Do you want egg and bacon or ham and cheese?'

'Neither. I just want to get home.'

He opened the egg and bacon box, stuffed a sandwich in his mouth and dumped everything else in her lap. 'You can feed me while I drive.'

Half an hour later, Ron glanced across at her. 'You're quiet. What's the matter? I thought you'd be pleased we're on our way to see our son.'

'I've been thinkin'.'

'And?'

'Jane suggested that if I didn't take the knife, perhaps Maureen had something to do with it. Perhaps she put it in my handbag. She had the chance when I went to the loo, just before I went out to meet Steve.' Beth grabbed

Ron's knee. 'It could be that she put the knife in my bag to make the fight worse.'

'That's possible, although I can't see why she'd do that.'

Beth frowned, rubbed her forehead and delved into her carrier bag for the tablets the prison doctor had prescribed. She took a couple and gulped them down with a swig from her water bottle. If only she could prove that Maureen had put the knife in her bag. But then, as Ron pointed out, what could Maureen have hoped to achieve? Was Beth expected to discover it and perhaps brandish it about during an alcohol-induced argument? Did Maureen think the police might get involved and that Beth would be arrested for causing an affray or something? What good would that be? Having never been in trouble before, she'd be let off with a caution and nothing would have changed, apart from the fact that she would have a criminal record. No, there had to be more to this. But what?

The more Beth thought about it, the more confused she became. She thought through Derek's latest evidence. He'd confirmed she was completely out of it when they'd carried her into Steve's. Whenever she'd had a couple of drinks and passed out before, she'd been unconscious for the rest of the night. So how and why had she come around, discovered a knife in her bag that she didn't know was there and then used it to stab Steve? What if she'd been right and it wasn't her that murdered Steve, but then who could it have been? She shook her head and sighed. What was it that kept floating into the edges of her consciousness? It had been there last night, just before the migraine struck...she gasped.

'What's up?'

'I think…I think Maureen gave me wine on purpose. She knew things between me and Steve got violent sometimes. She'd already told me the walls were thin and she'd heard us fightin'. That's why I got out before she reported me to Social Services. She could have guessed it was the wine that caused the row, or perhaps Mum said somethin'? She was always goin' on at me about drinkin' and getting violent. She could have let slip when Maureen rang her tryin' to find me. That's why Maureen gave me wine that night. I'm sure of it. She wanted me to fight with Steve.'

'But she thought you were seeing Jan.'

'She knew somehow.'

'Why would she want the two of you to fight?'

'Dunno. Perhaps she thought that I was about to move in with him and take Harrison with me. Not sure. I just know she did it. The more I think about the court case, the more I know she said those things on purpose. She wanted to make everythin' look really bad for me. We already know how much she enjoys havin' Harrison to herself.'

'I'm sure you've got something there, but I'm not sure how we'll ever prove it.'

He was right, of course he was.

'Wait, you remember Harrison said he woke up and he was lonely?'

'The night Maureen was in the shower.'

'What if she wasn't? Remember, Vic said the Morris had been moved overnight?'

'Where are you going with this?'

'What if…what if it wasn't me that murdered Steve. What if it was Maureen?'

'What? Where did that come from?'

'What if Maureen followed us back to Helston? What if she took the knife with her, murdered Steve – to stop me movin' in with him and takin' Harrison away from her – and framed me so she could have him all to herself?'

Ron braked hard and skidded into a layby. The tyres on the car following behind squealed as the driver swerved to avoid them, then blasted his horn and shook his fist as he went by.

Ron turned off the ignition. 'You're telling me that Maureen could have murdered Steve?'

'Everythin' fits. She plied me with wine, knowin' the effect it could have on me. Followed us back to Helston, murdered Steve – with her knife that she took to the scene – and planted my fingerprints on the knife while I was out of it.'

'But that would have meant her leaving Harrison alone in the house. Surely she wouldn't do that?'

'If she was prepared to murder, she'd do anything. Derek has confirmed I was comatose on arrival at Steve's. Harrison said he woke up and was lonely. You said yourself you were surprised that Maureen got cross when you asked her about it. And Vic said the car was moved overnight. Don't you see? It all fits? Please, Ron, let's go. Drive quickly. Our son's in the care of a murderer.'

The drive was unbearable. Neither spoke again until they turned into Emilia Boulevard. Before Ron could turn off the ignition, Beth had jumped out of the car, raced up the steps to the front door and pressed the doorbell. She held her ear close to the glass panel hoping to hear Harrison's excited voice. Nothing.

'Open the bleddy door!' Beth pressed the bell for the second time, and then a third, and then for good measure hammered on the doorframe.

Ron put his hand on Beth's shoulder. 'I'm not sure she's here, Beth. Look…the Morris is missing,'

'Not in?' A man's voice boomed behind her.

Beth jumped and spun around. Two uniformed police officers climbed the steps towards them.

'Sorry, Ma'mm, didn't mean to startle you,' the police officer smiled. 'I take it you're Mr and Mrs Taylor?

'That's right,' Beth replied. 'And you are…?'

'I'm Sergeant Todd, and this is PC Wright.' He pointed to his colleague on the step below him. 'We're here to speak to Mrs James.'

'Us too.' Beth pressed the bell once more but realised she was kidding herself. Maureen was definitely not here and, therefore, neither was Harrison. Disappointment flooded over her and her eyes filled with unshed tears. She bit her lip to stop them falling. She wasn't about to let down her guard in front of these two policemen.

'Have you still got your keys?' Ron asked.

Beth rushed back to Ron's car and grabbed the carrier bag Jane had handed to her as she was discharged. She delved into it, retrieved her house keys and raced back up the steps.

Her hand trembled as she tried to align the key with the lock, but eventually, it slipped into place and she pushed open the door. Beth raced up the stairs, followed by Ron, and burst into Harrison's room.

'She's taken him!' Beth screamed. 'His clothes have all gone, and his rabbit and his blanket.' She pointed to the wardrobe door, which swung open on its hinges to reveal empty clothes hangers. She sank to her knees and tugged open the bottom drawer. 'Everythin,' – all his stuff…it's gone. What's she done to him?' Beth angrily brushed aside the tears that ran down her cheeks.

Ron strode across the room and pulled her to her feet. She collapsed into his arms and the tears she'd been holding back flowed down her cheeks and dribbled from her chin. Ron took a handkerchief from his back pocket and wiped them gently away. His own eyes were also teary.

'Come on, darling, we'll find him. I promise you.' He patted her arm. Let's go back downstairs and talk to the police.'

The two policemen had waited in the hall. One was speaking on his mobile. 'Looks like she's done a runner, Chief. Taken the boy. An abduction case by the looks.' He paused to listen to the response. 'Okay, will do.'

'You have to find her!' Beth screamed. 'She's the one who murdered Steve. My son's been taken by a murderer.'

Sergeant Todd frowned. 'Murderer? Not sure about that, but we do need to talk to her. Come and sit yourself down.'

'But-'

'Let's sit.' Ron guided Beth to Maureen's chair, sat on the arm and put his hand on her shoulder.

'Thank you. Just to reassure you, CID are on their way. But while we wait for them, could you describe Mrs James's vehicle, and would you happen to know her registration number? We can get it from the DVLA, but it might speed things up if you have it?'

'It's a green Morris Minor Traveller,' Beth said. 'But I can't remember the number.'

'Me neither,' Ron shook his head.

Beth leapt to her feet. 'She may have some papers in the bureau. That is, if it's open. She normally keeps it locked.'

Beth rushed over to the corner of the room where the mahogany bureau stood. The key was in the lock. She opened the roll-top lid and began riffling.

'That's weird, an empty shoebox.' Beth tossed it to the floor, pulled out a pile of papers and shuffled through them.

'Here's something, what's this?' She returned to Ron and passed the paper to him.

'It's a speeding ticket,' Ron said. 'Crickey I never thought she had it in her.'

'But look at the date and the time. May 15$^{th}$ 8:55 p.m. The night Steve was stabbed to death. And the place...look, this is on the Helston Road. Vic was right, she was out in her car that night. She must have followed us. She *is* the murderer and *this* is absolute proof.'

Sergeant Todd stepped forward and held out his hand. 'We'll take that.'

Beth hesitated. 'I'm not sure.'

'It's okay, your lawyer will get a copy. But we need to get this processed.' He took the document from her. 'And who's this Vic you mentioned.'

'Vic Symonds. She lives next door, Flat Four. She thought Maureen may have used her car that night because the next day it was parked in a different place to her usual spot.'

'We'll get CID onto that as soon as they arrive.'

'What about my son? What are you doin' about gettin' him back?'

'We've already put out a search warrant for Mrs James and we'll get her registration number and vehicle details circulated. Let's have a cup of tea while we wait for CID to arrive. PC Wright makes an excellent brew.'

'Cup of tea? How can I sit here drinking bleddy tea?' Beth thumped her clenched fist against the seat cushion.

Ron stroked her shoulder. She could feel the tension lessen. She looked up and he smiled at her. Surely things would work out for the three of them. If there was any justice in the world, they simply had to.

PC Wright left the room and Beth could hear him rattling around in the kitchen. She knew she ought to offer to go and help but her legs didn't appear to be working properly.

'Try not to worry, we'll find him,' Sergeant Todd said.

They sat in silence until PC Wright returned with a tray and handed Beth a mug of strong, muddy-looking tea.

'Thanks,' she took a sip. 'Yuk, you've put sugar in it.'

PC Wright smiled. 'It's for the shock.' He reached over and offered her a plate of chocolate and wholemeal biscuits. 'For the energy.'

Beth accepted one mindlessly and took another sip of tea. Her head was spinning. Her hand shook as she put her mug on the coffee table.

Sergeant Todd stood, moved across the room and looked through the lounge window. This looks like CID now. I'll take my leave and give them a quick update on where we're at. PC Wright will stay with you until CID take over. Will you be okay for a few minutes?'

'We'll be fine, officer,' Ron said.

Beth watched him go. Today should have been amazing, the day she was reunited with Harrison – a dream come true. Now it was a nightmare.

What had Maureen done with their son?

# Chapter Twenty-five

Maureen glanced in her rear-view mirror. At least no one was following. But her stomach still clenched, those same severe cramps she used to experience when she was nursing Giles, especially after she discovered his infidelity, and again in the weeks following Anna's death. She simply had to ignore them and concentrate on her driving.

At least she'd had this escape route planned since before the court case. Thank goodness she hadn't cancelled the cottage rental. And what a relief that she'd had that phone call from the prison; otherwise the first thing she'd have known would have been Ron and Beth turning up on the front doorstep. But what on earth had happened? Why were they releasing Beth? Was there now some doubt about her guilt? Had the police found something out about Maureen's involvement? No wonder her stomach was giving her gip.

The narrow, winding roads didn't help. She found herself slowing down to a virtual standstill at each ninety-degree bend that she came to, so she could peer around them, hoping desperately that nothing was coming towards her. She was hopeless at reversing and there were very few passing places. This route was so typical of Cornish roads – a nightmare – but preferable to the main route. These roads might be tortuous, but at least it meant she didn't have to drive on the A30, which brought the risk of being spotted by cameras or police cars.

She relaxed a little as she came to a long straight length of road arched over by trees. The sunlight flickered through the golden leaves that remained on the deciduous trees, interspersed with the dark green foliage of the evergreens. The effect was similar to the strobe lights she and Giles used to enjoy dancing to at University parties – mesmerising.

She stopped at a cross roads and looked from left to right, and then checked again. The driver in the car behind her blasted his horn. How rude! She was only making sure that the crossing was safe.

'Are we nearly there?' Harrison wailed.

'Don't whinge, Harrison.'

'I want my daddy.'

'Stop it, Harrison. Stop it now!' She glanced in the rear-view mirror. Harrison was wiping tears from his cheek with his coat sleeve. He sniffed. Poor little mite. How could she have been so harsh?

'Don't cry Harrison. Look, I need to stop in the next village and shop for some food. I'll take you out of the car seat and you can lie down under the blanket. You'll be more comfortable. And if you're a really good boy and stay hidden, I'll bring you some chocolate.'

'Why I hide?'

'It's a game. Can you stay still and pretend you're Harry Potter under the invisibility cloak?'

She pulled up a little way past the village shop, not wanting an audience while she moved Harrison, then grabbed her handbag, a couple of bags and scrambled out of the car. She unclipped Harrison and helped him out of his seat.

'Lie down, sweetie, there's a good boy.' She covered him with the travel blanket. 'Keep this over you. Remember, you're Harry Potter, hiding, but you're only invisible while you stay under the blanket.'

Maureen locked the car door and entered the shop, grabbed a basket and filled it with food, drinks, cleaning products and toilet rolls. She should have brought more from home – emptied her kitchen cupboards as well as the pantry – but she'd been desperate to get away as quickly as she could.

She peeped out of the window to ensure Harrison was still out of sight, and then approached the checkout.

'Morning, my lover. Not seen you round 'ere before.' The shopkeeper peered over his glasses at her. They were rimmed with bright green plastic frames that Maureen decided clashed horribly with his red and white checked shirt. What was the saying? *Red and Green should never be seen?* A dark brown stain down his front looked like some sort of soup, or perhaps coffee? His aftershave was sickly, but no doubt masked far worse.

'Just passing through,' Maureen mumbled. She lifted her basket onto the counter.

'See you've got a beauty over there.' He indicated out of the window with his thumb.

Maureen's stomach cramped again. She looked over his shoulder, half expecting to see Harrison waving to her. She breathed a sigh of relief as she realised he was referring to the Morris. She should have parked further away. What if he'd seen her moving Harrison from his seat? Would he report her for leaving a small child unattended? Would he remember her once the police inevitably started looking for them? She picked up a bag of chocolate drops from the tray on the counter and added it to her basket.

'That will be all, thank you.'

She paid in cash and left the shop without another word. She could feel the shopkeeper's eyes boring into her back as she rushed to the Morris, fumbled with the lock and sank into the driver's seat. This was a mistake; she wouldn't come here again. After today, she'd have to find somewhere that provided a home delivery service. Giles's Morris Minor Traveller was far too distinctive to risk driving it again.

'Are you alright, Harrison?'

Her question was met with silence, apart from Harrison's steady breathing. He must have dropped off to sleep.

She turned the key in the ignition and looked back towards the shop. The shopkeeper stood at the window, watching her. She released the handbrake and began to pull away, narrowly missing a young man on a bicycle who was riding past her.

'I'm so sorry!' she called through the window.

The youth stuck two fingers up at her and carried on.

Oh dear, this was not what she'd planned. The idea had been to disappear, not create havoc so that people would remember her. The police search was probably already underway. After all, Beth and Ron could be back at her empty house around about now. No doubt they would report Harrison missing and the police would immediately start searching for them both.

She drove along the road, which led to the small hamlet where she'd stayed as a child. They'd always stayed in a caravan on the farmer's field nearby, but she remembered passing by the rental cottage on their way to the beach. It always reminded her of the picture on a box of biscuits they'd been given by Aunt Belinda one Christmas. The house was stone built, with leaded windows and wisteria growing all over it. Of course, the wisteria would not be in flower now, but she was sure the cottage would still look very pretty.

Her heart leapt as she recognised the turnoff track that led to the cottage. She flipped on her indicator, but realised with a start that she'd turned the window wipers on instead. Flustered, she tried again, this time successfully, and fortunately there was no one behind her. The car bounced down the track for several hundred yards before the familiar cottage of her childhood appeared before her.

It was much smaller than she remembered but, although the wisteria was bare, as she'd known it would be, there were numerous border flowers still in full bloom and it looked just as pretty as in her memory. The house was surrounded by trees, including a huge Eucalyptus tree that towered above them. She spotted a wooden garage in front of the tree and pulled up before it. She'd put the car inside, out of sight, as soon as she'd unpacked it.

'We're here, Harrison. On our holiday.'

Maureen opened her door and got out. She flicked her seat forward so that Harrison could clamber over from the back. Maureen held out her arm to steady him as he climbed out of the car, rubbing his eyes and yawning.

'Is Daddy here?'

'He's had to go away for a while.'

'Is he in prison?'

'It's to do with his work. He'll be back in a couple of weeks.'

Harrison raced towards the front door of the cottage.

'Wait for me, Harrison. I need to find the key.' She rifled through her handbag, found her key ring, crunched her way along the gravel pathway and opened the front door. They stepped into a small hallway with flagstone floors, white walls and a wooden staircase. 'Okay, Harrison, let's explore.'

Harrison ran in front and gasped with excitement as he entered each room. To the left of the front door they discovered the dining area, which led into the kitchen with oak cupboards and an old-fashioned butler sink. On the right-hand side of the house, the lounge looked warm and cosy, with a cast iron wood burning stove. The room had a pale cream carpet, mostly covered by a large Persian rug in a burgundy, cream and dark blue pattern. Upstairs, two bedrooms led off of the hallway: one with a double bed and one with two singles, all covered with Cornish tartan bedspreads and cushions to match. The rooms, both painted white, had cream carpets, the same as the lounge. The bathroom had an oak floor and a white bathroom suite which included a roll top bath and a walk-in shower. The walls were also painted white, with white tiles around the bath and hand-basin. Fluffy yellow towels of various sizes hung over a stainless-steel towel-rail. The whole house smelt of wax furniture polish and lavender.

'I think we will like it here, don't you, Harrison?'

Harrison nodded.

'Let's unpack our things and then we'll have dinner. What would you like?'

'Sausage, mashed potatoes and peas, please.'

'Didn't we have that last night?'

'I like it,' Harrison stuffed his hands in his coat pocket and pretended to sulk.

'Okay, but we'll have something else tomorrow. Perhaps chicken and broccoli?'

Harrison nodded again.

The unpacking didn't take long. Maureen parked the Morris in the garage and promised herself that this would be where it stayed for the next four months. She wasn't quite sure what was going to happen once her letting came to an end in early March. The agent had warned her that the cottage was already fully booked for the summer season. The only certainty was that they would need to move on at that time. She pushed her concerns aside; there was plenty of time to worry about all that later. At least the cottage had a phone, so she could order food deliveries, and she had plenty of cash left. She didn't want to use her bank account or mobile phone; she'd watched that female police detective, Vera, on the TV and knew the police could trace people's location if their mobile was switched on. Thank goodness hers had been switched off since before she'd left Emilia Boulevard.

'Tomorrow, if the weather's okay, we'll take you for a walk through the woods to the beach. I used to visit there to build sandcastles when I was a child. I also took my daughter there when she was your age. She loved it, and it's not far.'

'Do they have ice cream?'

'Not sure. But, if not, I'll order some when I do a telephone shop tomorrow. I hope I can find someone like Mr Price who'll deliver to the door. Let's light the fire and then we'll cook our dinner.'

Harrison raced across to the basket of wood and held up the biggest log he could find.

'Perfect,' she said. 'Everything's going to be just perfect.'

# Chapter Twenty-six

There was a tap on the front door.

Beth stiffened.

Ron squeezed Beth's shoulder. 'Come on in!' he shouted.

Two men in dark grey suits entered. 'Good afternoon, Mr and Mrs Taylor. I'm DCI Sweeny and this is DS Smith.' The Inspector reached over and shook their hands. He turned to PC Wright. 'We'll take it from here, thanks. Your Sergeant is waiting for you in the car.'

'Okay, Guv. Bye, you two.' He nodded towards Beth and Ron and raised his hand in a wave as he left the room. The door slammed as he left the house.

Once settled on the sofa, DCI Sweeny smiled. 'Sergeant Todd has brought us up to scratch on the abduction of your son and also on the speeding ticket I understand you discovered. I'm afraid we need to ask you a few more questions.'

'What about Harrison? He's in danger and you're just sittin' here asking questions. You should be out there lookin' for him.' Beth could feel the panic rising from her stomach. She stifled a sob.

'And these questions will help us to find him. I can assure you that things are already in motion. An Incident Room is being set up at Falmouth Police Station and we'll be joined shortly by PC Thompson.'

'More police, more questions. Don't you understand, my son's life is in the hands of a madwoman.' Beth pulled a tatty paper handkerchief from her sleeve and rubbed her eyes.

'Mrs Taylor...or may I call you Beth?'

'I don't care what you call me and I don't care what you think of me, I just need you to get out there and find Harrison.' Beth's voice cracked.

Ron pulled her close and stroked her head. 'Who is this PC Thompson? My wife has a point...the more of you we have here, the fewer there are out there looking for our son.'

'I know neither of you has met her before, but PC Thompson has been appointed as your Family Liaison Officer. Actually, she's volunteered, having met your son previously. She took a bit of a shine to him, apparently. Bonny lad, by all accounts.' He looked around the room. 'Is that his photo on the bureau?'

'Taken on his third birthday, last June,' Beth mumbled through her tears. Despite her anguish, her heart swelled with pride.

'You'll get it back, but we need to get his picture copied and circulated. The Super's already trying to book a spot on Crimestoppers.' He took the photograph and slipped it into his briefcase.

'Please...please promise me you'll get him back. *He's my life.*' Beth turned to Ron and reached for his hand. '*Our* life.'

'We have no reason to believe Mrs James will do Harrison any harm. She's driving a very distinctive vehicle and she won't be able to leave Cornwall without us picking her up on CCTV. I have every confidence that he'll be back with you within the next twenty-four hours. Hopefully, a lot less.' He took out his pocketbook and pencil. 'Now, let's recap on where we're at. I understand, Mrs Taylor – sorry, Beth, that you were released on parole this afternoon?'

Gosh, was it only a few hours ago? It felt like ages.

'That's because I'm innocent. She's the one that should be arrested for murder. You should lock her up and throw away the key for what she's done to me.' She looked up at Ron and squeezed his hand. 'Done to us.'

'Try not to worry. They'll show up soon. You can't go to ground for long without needing to use your mobile or pay for food. We're keeping a check on her accounts. Her vehicle is our best bet – it's so distinctive. It's only a matter of time until we get a sighting.' He wrote something down in his notebook and then turned his attention back to Beth. 'And when you got here, Mrs James had packed up and gone, taking Harrison with her? Did she know you were on your way back?'

Beth blew her nose, dabbed her eyes and sniffed. 'The prison officer told me they had to check out my parole address with Maureen. Apparently, that's normal procedure. So, she would have been warned.'

'Have either of you any idea why that would encourage her to abduct Harrison?'

'It's probably my fault,' Ron said. 'I told her that when Beth was released, we were looking to set up home together.' He glanced down at Beth and squeezed her shoulder. 'We've been estranged for a while. I tried to reassure her that she would still be part of Harrison's life, but she may not have believed me. She's totally obsessive about him. I think it comes from losing her daughter and grandson a few years back.' Ron stroked Beth's arm. 'I'm sorry.'

Beth rested her head against him. 'It wasn't your fault. Don't make excuses for her. She's pure evil. She knew we'd catch on eventually. But there's no reason she should take it out on Harrison. Why would she take him from us like this?'

'Is there anywhere you can think of where she may have gone?' DCI Sweeny asked.

'No idea,' Ron said.

Beth shook her head.

'And the speeding ticket? The time and location could be evidence to suggest that Mrs James may have followed you on the night of the murder. Did you have any suspicion about that?'

'None at all. I was totally out of it. I remember Steve turned up late. I gave him short shift, and then…nowt after that until I woke the next mornin'. I left Maureen here in charge of Harrison. It wasn't until this bloke turned up and said I had to be carried into Steve's that I remembered what Vic – my next-door neighbour – said about the Morris not bein' in its usual place the next day. I never dreamt that she'd leave Harrison alone. But then I realised that if she was at Steve's at the time of the murder, it could have been her that took the knife to his house and used it to murder Steve.'

Ron turned to DCI Sweeny. 'Do you believe she could have murdered him?'

'The discovery of the speeding ticket certainly makes her a person of interest.'

'My son's been abducted by a murderer.' Beth burst into tears.

'Come on, darling,' Ron knelt beside the chair and wrapped his arms around her. 'You know how much she loves him. She won't hurt him.'

'You're right, sir. I'm sure he's not at risk. He'll soon be back with you both, where he belongs.' He looked up as there was a tap on the door. 'That'll be PC Thompson. I'll go.' He came back into the room accompanied by a young woman. Beth put her at about twenty-seven. She wore a smart grey skirt, white blouse, black tights and shoes and her long dark hair was scraped back in a ponytail.

'Hi there, I'm PC Thompson, otherwise known as Nicky. I'll be spending the night with you tonight. Don't worry about finding me somewhere to sleep. I'll be fine on the sofa. I'm your link with Head Office and the Incident Room, which is currently being set up in the Falmouth Police Station. Don't be afraid to ask me any questions or tell me anything you may think could be relevant – no matter how insignificant.' She smiled and Beth instantly warmed to her. 'I met your son and I will do anything – anything I can – to help you get him back.'

'We all will, I can assure you,' DCI Sweeny smiled at Beth. 'DS Smith, can you nip back to the car and grab a couple of evidence boxes to pack up Mrs James's paperwork from the bureau? I'll just have a quick look around her bedroom and then we'll leave you in peace. We'll go next door and see your neighbour.' He glanced at his notebook. 'Vic Symonds? And then we'll go back to the police station. If you want us for anything, just tell PC Thompson. Anytime, day or night. Obviously, if anything changes or we get any news, we'll be in touch.'

Beth wanted to trust them; she really did. But Harrison was her son. Their son. Yet here they were, the pair of them, having to just sit here drinking tea and hoping other people, strangers, would get their son back for them. It didn't feel right. It didn't feel anything like enough.

# Chapter Twenty-seven

Maureen switched on the TV. She staggered back and collapsed onto the sofa as her photograph filled the screen. Another picture of Giles's Morris Minor, or one identical to it, followed. The camera then focussed on a man. A red label footer on the screen identified him as DCI Sweeny.

'We are currently looking for this woman, Maureen James.' The photograph of Maureen appeared again on the board behind DCI Sweeny. 'We believe her to be accompanied by this three-year-old boy, Harrison Taylor.' A new picture was displayed beside Maureen's, this time of Harrison, the one taken on his recent birthday. 'We urgently need to trace them both. We believe they are travelling in a dark green Morris Minor Traveller, similar to this one, with the registration number 654 CCV.' DCI Sweeney pointed back to the photograph of a Morris Minor Traveller. 'If you have any information, please contact us at the number on the screen. Thank you. I will not be taking questions at this time.'

Oh, my God! Maureen clutched her chest as her heart raced. She'd been right, the Morris was an absolute giveaway. Thank goodness she'd hidden it in the garage. How on earth had they got a photograph of her? She never had photographs taken and, anyway, that one had been so formal. Her head spun as she thought through the possibilities. Of course, it was the picture from her driving licence. The police must have got it from the DVLA.

'Nana Mo!'

'Coming, Harrison. Wait there for me. You're not used to these stairs.'

The last thing she needed right now was Harrison asking why he was on the telly. She switched off the TV and stood. Her hip clicked and the pain shot down her leg. She groaned and limped towards the stairs. 'Coming!'

Harrison stood on the top step.

'What matter, Nana Mo?'

'It's my leg, darling. Don't worry, I'm just getting old. Can't get up the stairs as quickly as I used to.'

She reached his side, clutched his hand and helped him down the steps. 'Time for breakfast. Do you want cereal or toast?'

'I prefer cereal, please.'

'Good boy. *Prefer*. That's a good word. Well done.' She handed Harrison his bowl of cereal.

'Nana Mo? Harry at school today?'

'We're on holiday, so no school for a while.'

'I promise Isaac we play football today.'

'I'll play with you later.'

'I want to play with Isaac.' He pushed his cereals away, stuck out his bottom lip and threw his spoon across the table. 'Don't want any more.'

'Don't do that, sweetie. You need to eat, or you'll have no energy.'

Harrison got down from the table, marched into the lounge and switched on the TV. Maureen followed him, concerned that he might see the news channel. That would take some explaining. She watched as he pressed various buttons on the remote. *Peter Rabbit* filled the screen while Harrison threw himself onto the sofa.

How did he work these things out? He was only three for goodness sake. And why was he in such a bad mood? It wasn't like him to sulk.

Best to leave him be for now, she decided.

She walked back into the kitchen and picked up her mug of coffee. Perhaps his mood will improve after zoning out on *Peter Rabbit* for a while.

Today was a bit of a wakeup call. What was she going to do to keep him occupied? He was used to a busy social life at nursery school three days a week. He spent evenings and weekends with his dad, who kept him active with sports, walks, rock-pooling and visits to the cinema. How could she possibly fill the gap created by bringing him here – especially now she daren't use the car to take him anywhere? She pushed the worries to the back of her mind and picked up the visitor file. Turning the pages illustrating *Local Walks and Places to Visit,* she came to the one headed *Shopping*. Half way down the page was a section labelled *Groceries delivered to your door.* Thank goodness for that. And with a delivery charge of only three pounds – even cheaper than Mr Price. She sat at the kitchen table and began to write her list.

Beth walked into the kitchen as Ron shoved his mobile into his back pocket. 'Morning darling. Come and sit down. Did you get any sleep?'

'You're jokin'. Any news?'

'I've been getting an update from Nicky. They haven't found Harrison yet, but they're sure Maureen hasn't left

Cornwall. They've checked the toll bridge, the ferry in Plymouth and the cameras on the A30 and A38. No sightings so far. I've also been onto my boss. I told him what's going on and that I wouldn't be in. He was pretty good about it. Offered me compassionate leave.'

'How can you sound so calm? What if Maureen's harmed him? The more I think about it, the more positive I am that she must have murdered Steve. It's the only explanation that makes any sense. She's clearly mentally unstable.'

'She won't do anything to harm Harrison. She adores him.'

Of course, Ron was right, but Maureen wasn't used to driving. What if they were involved in an accident?

'I've made us all a pot of tea,' Ron said softly.

'Tea? How can I sit here drinkin' tea? We need to find Harrison.'

'Nicky assured me the police are taking this *very* seriously. They'll be doing everything they can.'

'But they haven't found him yet, have they? I can't just sit here waitin' for news. We have to do somethin' or I'll go mad.'

Ron poured her a mug and handed her a plate of buttered toast. 'Eat. You need to keep up your energy levels.'

'We need to get out there and help with the search. But then, what if we go out and Maureen decides to come back?'

'The way she's emptied the wardrobes and pantry I'd say she has no intention of returning. She's gone to ground somewhere. Nicky!' Ron shouted in the direction of the lounge. 'I've made some tea and toast. Do you want to join us?'

Nicky poked her head around the door. 'Hi there. I'd love to. As long as you're sure I'm not in the way?'

'Ron tells me there's no news yet,' Beth said.

Nicky perched on a chair, reached for a slice of toast and shook her head. 'Not yet, but we'll find them. Try not to worry.'

'How can I not? There must be things we can do to support the police effort, surely. I thought perhaps we could get some missin' posters made up from his birthday photograph. I've still got my copy. Then we could distribute them to post offices and shops, especially in the small villages. If Maureen's gone to ground in Cornwall, I'm guessin' it'll be somewhere off the beaten track. We could get some to Jan – that's a friend of mine who drives a taxi in Truro – I'm sure she'll help.' Beth foraged in her carrier bag and pulled out the photograph of Harrison holding his birthday cake. 'Here...we can use this.'

'I'll check with DCI Sweeny, but I can't see any problems with any of that.' Nicky took a slice of toast, pulled out her mobile from the back pocket of her skirt and walked back into the lounge.

Beth could hear her talking, presumably to the Incident Room. 'What do you think, Ron? It's got to be better than just sittin' here all day, waitin' for the phone to ring. We could add the details of her vehicle and registration number. As Nicky said, her Morris Minor's quite distinctive.'

'I think it's a good idea, as long as the police agree to it. But first you need to eat, and then, if we get the okay from Nicky, we'll get off to the printers. You can ring Jan while we're in the car.'

'I'll also put somethin' out on Facebook, WhatsApp and Messenger. I know the police use Social Media – I've seen messages before – but I'd hate to think we'd missed somethin'.'

'It'll be okay, Beth.' Ron held out a piece of toast to her. 'He'll be back with us in no time. Here, you must keep your strength up.'

Beth took the toast and bit into it while scrolling through Facebook on her phone. Somebody must have seen them. Someone must know where they are.

# Chapter Twenty-eight

Maureen sank onto the smooth boulder that nestled beneath the cliffs. The rock was warm from the mid-morning sun, and its position gave her some protection from the cool easterly wind. She slipped her shoes off, brushed the sand from her feet and watched Harrison as he picked up small stones from the shoreline and hurled them into the sea. Plop, plop.

'Look, Nana Mo, I can throw *really* far!'

'Well done, but don't get too close to the water. Why don't you come back up here and finish building your castle?' Maureen had been relieved to discover a bucket and spade set in the hall cupboard the previous night. She wasn't sure that the online delivery service would stock such things out of season, and besides, ordering children's toys might cause someone to ask questions.

Harrison shrugged his shoulders. 'Okay.' He walked towards her and slumped to his knees beside the blue plastic bucket, used the spade to fill it with the damp sand and then patted the top to flatten it.

'That's right, Harrison. Now flip it over as quickly as you can.'

Harrison grunted as he struggled to lift the bucket and turn it over. Some sand spilled out in the process, but the remainder created a passable – if slightly wonky – castle.

'That's lovely, Harrison. Try another one.'

Maureen leaned back against the warm rocks, breathed in the familiar smell of the sea air and lifted her bare feet onto a conveniently positioned boulder.

She looked up as two seagulls squabbled, squawked and screeched while they circled above her, fighting over a fish that dangled from the beak of the smaller bird.

She loved this beach. She thought back to the happy holidays she'd spent here with her parents.

There'd been very few other times in her childhood that she could even begin to describe as happy, but somehow, her mum and dad always seemed more relaxed here. The atmosphere was always calmer than back at home in their two-bedroomed, dilapidated council house in Fulham. It seemed as though the sun had shone every day. They'd brought picnics to this very beach and her dad made sandcastles, which she dressed in shells. Such happy memories, only to be dashed after they returned home and the usual abuse began again.

Not that her dad had ever been violent towards either her or her mum. Not physically that is. Verbally, now that was a different issue. He would shout obscenities and criticise both of them on a daily basis. He would never allow either of them any spending money, or permit them to invite friends around, or go out of the house without him. Even when she started school, her dad would drop her at the school gate in the morning and he'd be there waiting for her when she finished. No sleepovers for Maureen. The only person who was ever allowed to visit was Aunt Belinda, her dad's sister who lived nearby, and that was only on rare occasions and always under her dad's supervision.

One night, the rows had got louder and more violent than ever. Maureen cowered under her duvet as her dad bellowed and her mum screamed, over and over again. Maureen prayed. *Please stop. Please make them stop.* The words crowded her mind. She had no idea who she was praying to. She had never been to church, and her only knowledge of Christ was the nativity play at school when she'd played the part of a shepherd. She auditioned for the part of Mary, but that had been awarded to the teacher's pet, the beautiful Miriam. Of course it had. Miriam was always first in the queue for absolutely everything.

The sobbing had stopped with a strangled scream.

'Mummy?' Maureen had shouted as she ran into her parents' bedroom.

She stopped dead in her tracks. Her mum lay on her side, her eyes wide open, her body perfectly still. She was wearing her pale green paisley dress. Maureen hated that dress; the colour didn't suit her mum and it had a hole in the sleeve. Now it was ripped down the front and covered in blood. The room smelled of her mum's cheap perfume and a sickening sweet metallic scent.

'Dad?'

'She was going to leave me. I couldn't-' His voice caught as tears flowed unchecked down his face.

'Is she dead?'

'Get out. Go to Aunt Belinda's. Go now!'

Maureen dragged her eyes away from her dead mum. She knew she was dead because her eyes, though open, were glazed over. Just like her dog, Lucy, when she'd been put to sleep by the vet. She raced down the stairs, stood on her tippy toes to reach the latch, opened the front door and ran.

She didn't stop until she got to Aunt Belinda's house and rang the doorbell.

'My goodness, Maureen. Where's your coat?' Her aunt frowned. 'And why no shoes? Your feet are filthy.'

'Mum's dead. Mum's dead!' Maureen screamed, before bursting into tears.

'What are you on about, child? Get inside.' Aunt Belinda grabbed Maureen's shoulder, pulled her inside and slammed the door. 'Stop snivelling. Go and sit in the lounge.' Her aunt followed her. 'Now calm down and tell me what's happened?'

Maureen perched on her aunt's cold leather sofa. She longed for a cuddle, a hug, but none was forthcoming. Maureen couldn't remember her aunt ever offering her any affection. She was so like her father – cold as ice – and she clearly wasn't about to change her habits, not even tonight when Maureen most needed it.

'Maureen, I'm waiting.'

'It's Mum. Dad stabbed her.'

'Is she dead?'

Maureen nodded.

'I'd better ring the police.' She turned and walked back into the hall, leaving Maureen to sob uncontrollably.

The police found the front door open. In her haste, Maureen had failed to pull it shut behind her. They entered the house and discovered her dad's body lying next to her mum's. He'd taken his own life and condemned her to a miserable, loveless life growing up with her aunt.

Aunt Belinda had never let Maureen forget how much she was in her debt, although Maureen had never actually worked out quite why she should be grateful. Grateful for what?

Maureen had never been back to this beach, with all its happy memories, until after Anna was born. Giles brought her here, not long after Anna started walking. They brought a picnic and a big travel rug and Anna would totter from each one to the other, crossing back and forth over the rug with tiny steps, giggling with joy at her own achievement. Anna hadn't even been twelve months old – not quite. She was always well advanced for her age, very creative and extremely bright. Who knows what she would have achieved if she'd gone to university instead of leaving school to be with that waste-of-space husband of hers? She'd have been a good mother. An even better mother than Beth was with Harrison.

Maureen woke with a start. 'Harrison?' She looked around, raised her voice and shouted. 'Harrison, where are you?'

No one answered, except for a single seagull that squawked laughingly at her panic as she scanned the empty beach.

Maureen staggered along the shoreline. Her feet felt like lead, her heart thumped so loudly, and painfully, she was sure she was having a heart attack. My God, everything she'd done to keep Harrison to herself and now one careless moment and he was gone.

'Harrison!'

Tears poured down her cheeks. Had he been knocked off his feet by a wave and swept out to sea? She imagined the cold water closing over his head, Harrison struggling as he opened his mouth to shout for her, salty water cascading down his throat, suffocating the precious life out of him. Or, perhaps even worse, had he been snatched? He was such a good-looking boy and so innocent, she couldn't even think about it.

'Harrison!' she screamed.

'Nana Mo!'

Maureen looked across to the beach café, from where Harrison's voice had come from. He sat at an outside table waving to her.

'Oh, Harrison.' Maureen raced across the sand, threw her arms around him and kissed the top of his head. 'Why did you go off like that? I was so worried about you.'

'We came for ice cream, didn't we, Harrison?'

Maureen looked up into the cold eyes of a woman, probably in her fifties, with short blonde hair, wearing cream linen trousers, a white shirt and a red anorak.

'Harrison was alone and I was worried about his safety. So I brought him here for an ice cream. I figured you'd turn up eventually.'

'But you must have seen me over there, at the other end of the beach sitting on the rocks. Couldn't you have brought him over to me?'

'You should be grateful I didn't ring the police and report you. You're not fit to look after a child. You're old enough to know you can't take your eyes off them. What would his mother say?'

This was all she needed. A report to the police would quickly bring them running. Maureen knew they'd be looking for them both by now. She needed to divert attention away and diffuse this situation as quickly as possible.

'I'm sorry, I wasn't feeling too well...I must have... Come on, Harrison, let's be getting off. We've got a long drive back home. Thank you so much for looking after him. Say goodbye to the nice lady, and thank you.'

'Tank you for ice cream.'

Maureen grabbed Harrison's hand and steered him back down the beach.

'Never, ever wander off like that again, Harrison. You frightened me half to death. Someone could have snatched you and stolen you away. We wouldn't want that to happen, now would we?'

'Harry not get stolen. Daddy show me. I shout "Stranger Danger" and then kick, like this.' Harrison kicked over the remnants of his sandcastle. 'Then I run, like this.' He raced to the edge of the footpath that led to the cottage.

'Wait for me, Harrison.' Maureen raced after him, puffing and panting as she reached his side.

What a day, and it wasn't over yet. She hoped tomorrow would be a bit easier.

# Chapter Twenty-nine

Beth answered her mobile on the second ring. 'Nicky, tell me it's good news.'

'Sorry, I didn't mean to get your hopes up, but I promised to ring after we took up the issue that we discussed last night, and checked out holiday lets. It was a good idea, but I'm afraid we didn't find any long or short rentals taken out this past week. We've also checked hotels and guest houses. Nothing. We've got a member of the team working his way through B&B's.'

'What about her mobile or bank?'

'She's probably got enough cash with her to get through these first few days and her mobile is switched off, but we still think someone will spot her vehicle before long. I'll keep you informed.'

Beth sighed and leaned back in her seat. 'That was Nicky. No news as of yet.'

'So I gathered. But at least we've made good progress. I couldn't believe the printers were able to rattle off those two hundred posters within the hour.'

Beth's mobile pinged with an incoming text. She glanced at the screen.

'And Jan's a star. She says she's already got one poster displayed in every Truro taxi, and all the drivers have agreed to take a few to distribute. We only dropped them off with her half an hour ago.'

'Where next?'

Beth opened her map and traced her finger along the Helston Road. 'If you follow the signs into the town, we can park up and hit the main street. Then we can go to the supermarket and ask if they'll put up a poster. We could also grab a sandwich for you. Knowing you, you'll be hungry by then.'

Ron laughed. 'How well you know me. But do you think she'd risk going into a big town like Helston?'

'I know it's unlikely, but lots of people go into town from the surroundin' small villages and hamlets for shoppin' or the likes. If they see the posters, they might recognise Harrison, or the Morris, and come forward.' Beth glanced back at her map. 'After Helston, we could carry on towards Porthleven. I think from memory there are a couple of local shops along the way that might agree to a poster. Porthleven attracts lots of visitors – even out of season – and then we could carry onto Praa Sands. They've got a small shop and a pub overlookin' the beach, with several caravan parks nearby.'

Beth and Ron walked down from the car park and entered the small town of Porthleven. The tide was out and the small boats rested on the sandy floor of the inner harbour. Noisy seagulls circled above them, occasionally landing on the harbour wall across from the pub. Even though it was Autumn, it was sunny and quite warm. Several people sat at the tables eating fish and chips, or crab sandwiches, while the birds kept a close eye on the customers, just waiting for an opportunity to pounce on the food.

'Do you remember the last time we were here?' Beth asked.

'Of course. You told me you were pregnant, and I asked you to marry me.'

'I thought you'd run a mile.'

Ron grabbed her hand and squeezed it. 'No chance.'

'You've been so supportive. I want you to know... whatever happens, I do appreciate what you've done for us both, and...how much I've missed you.'

Ron pulled her to face him, wrapped his arms around her and kissed her tenderly. 'I love you both. Now, let's go and find our son and start our life as a family over again.'

Ron and Beth wandered along the main street, calling in at small shops and restaurants. Everyone agreed to display a poster and wished them well in their search.

'Where next?' Ron asked as they left the last restaurant.

'Praa Sands, I guess.'

They began to walk back to the car when a voice halted them in their tracks.

'Hello there!'

Ron and Beth turned around to see a man running towards them. He was about fifty, slim, and was wearing a yachting jacket.

'Are you the couple looking for the young boy and the Morris Traveller?'

Beth's heart leapt. 'Have you seen him?'

'My son had a close encounter with a dark green Morris yesterday. Some woman was driving, pulled out without looking and almost knocked him off his bike. I remember him saying about the Morris. They're quite rare, especially in that original dark green colour.'

'Did she have our little boy with her?' Beth asked.

'Danny said she was alone.' He looked at Beth. 'I'm sorry. It may not have been the same vehicle, but I thought it was worth mentioning.'

'Thank you so much,' said Ron. 'Where did this happen?'

'A small village on the north coast called Rowenan. Do you know it?'

'We'll find it. Thanks again.'

Beth and Ron raced back to the car.

'You'd better ring Nicky and update her,' Ron said, as he pulled out of the car park. 'I assume we're off to Rowenan now?'

She nodded.

Beth thought through all the possible reasons why Maureen, if it was her, could be on her own. Had she left Harrison alone again? Had she harmed him? Was he dead in a ditch somewhere? Tears rolled down her cheeks and the lump in her throat threatened to choke her. A sob escaped, despite her efforts to suppress it.

Ron glanced across at her. 'Don't worry darling. 'There'll be a simple explanation for her being alone. Maybe he just didn't notice. He was taking evasive action at the time after all.'

'You think it was her then?'

Ron nodded.

Beth wiped her tears away, cleared her throat, picked up her mobile and tapped in the now familiar number. 'Nicky?' Beth held her mobile close to her ear. 'I'm putting you on speaker so Ron can hear. We've just had someone tell us that a dark green Morris Traveller was seen in the village of Rowenan.'

'I'll tell DCI Sweeny immediately. He'll no doubt get a couple of patrol cars over there.'

'We're heading over in that direction now ourselves. Any other news?' Beth asked.

'I'm not sure I should tell you this, but we've had a call from someone called Derek Jenson who lives in Helston. He's the guy that helped carry you into Steve's on the night of the murder. He saw your poster in Helston. He didn't think anything at the time, but the poster reminded him that he saw a vehicle like Maureen's parked in the road, just down from Steve's, and that there was an elderly lady sat in it. He's coming into the Incident Room to see if he can identify Mrs James, but it looks as though his statement will confirm that she was at the murder scene at the time of the murder.'

'Does that mean I'm off the hook?'

'Early days yet, Beth. We need to interview her, but it's looking hopeful. Keep in touch.'

Ron looked across at her, smiled and winked.

Beth slid her mobile into the back pocket of her jeans. 'Will it take us long to get there?'

'We should be there by half three. That still gives us a good couple of hours before we lose the light.'

Beth leaned back, closed her eyes and yawned. Last night's lack of sleep was catching up with her. How she yearned for this to be a family drive, on a visit to the beach for a picnic.

'Ron!'

'Christ, Beth! You made me jump.'

'I've just remembered…Maureen showed me a photograph that she kept in the bureau. She was tellin' me about Giles and how they used to take Anna for picnics at a small cove on the north coast. Anna was in the photograph. She mentioned the name, but I'm damned if I can think of it.'

'It may come back to you as we drive around, but you'd better mention it to Nicky. They have all the papers from the bureau at the Incident Room. It may be that one of the team could identify it.'

Beth's heart raced as they drove into Rowenan and pulled up outside the village shop.

'Let's try in here first,' Ron said.

They entered the shop, pausing for their eyesight to adjust to the low light. The shopkeeper stood behind his counter with his back to the window, leafing through some paperwork.

He looked up over his bright green plastic-framed glasses and smiled. 'Afternoon. Not seen you around 'ere before, my lovelies. Can I help you?'

Beth moved closer and handed him one of the posters. 'We wondered if you've seen this boy? He would have been with a pensioner, who he calls Nana Mo. She would have been drivin' a dark green Morris Minor Traveller.'

'I saw her yesterday. Couldn't help but notice the vehicle. But I didn't see the young lad.'

Beth sighed. 'Did you see which way she went?'

'Drove off towards St Piran. Nearly cleared up a young lad in the process. Pulled out just as 'e was passing.'

'Thanks. Could you put this poster up for us?' Beth pushed it towards him.

He nodded and took it from her. 'Good luck. If you find this Nana Mo, could you ask if I can have first refusal on that Morris?'

Beth clambered into the car and fastened her seat belt. It pulled tight across her chest. Feeling like she might suffocate, she wound down the window and gasped for air.

You okay?' Ron asked.

'Panic attack.' She swallowed and breathed deeply, in through the nose and out through the mouth. Little by little the vice loosened. 'How come neither this bike rider nor the shopkeeper saw Harrison? What has she done to him?' She looked out through the open window but saw nothing; her eyes filled with tears.

'Don't give up hope. Not now we're so close to finding him.' Ron took her hand. 'We will find him, I know we will.'

'And I can't believe that guy.' Beth raged. 'Expectin' us to help him buy a bleddy car.'

'At least he confirmed we're getting close.'

They drove to the village of St Piran and circled back and forth for the next couple of hours, peering into car parks and drives, turning down cul-de-sacs and exploring minor roads. Eventually, the light failed them and it became impossible to continue.

Ron pulled up at the side of the road and turned towards Beth. 'What do you want to do?'

'Other than find Harrison?' She looked at Ron and saw the hurt in his eyes. 'Sorry, I didn't mean to sound sarcastic. What did you mean?'

'We could go back to Emilia Boulevard, or we could check-in for the night at that pub we spotted twenty minutes ago. That way we could start tomorrow's search as soon as it's light enough.'

Beth sighed. 'I suppose that makes sense.'

'One bed or two?'

'I could do with a cuddle.'

'You'd better give Nicky a ring and let her know where we'll be.'

Beth reached for her phone and tapped in Nicky's number. 'Nicky, it's us. We're calling it a night and staying at the Blue Lion in St Piran until first light tomorrow morning. Has anyone been able to identify that cove in the photograph yet?'

'Sorry Beth, not yet. But we've managed to track down one of the Coastal Path wardens – he works for the Council. He's coming in first thing tomorrow morning to see if he can recognise it. We'll be in touch as soon as he's been in.'

'Thanks. Goodnight.'

'Goodnight and try not to worry. We're close to finding them now.'

Beth slipped her mobile into her pocket and glanced across at Ron.

He smiled at her. 'Let's have a drink in the bar and something to eat. We can check with the locals and see if anyone's seen them or the Morris.'

Beth's head spun as she got out of the car. She clutched the door for support.

Ron rushed to her side, held her arm and supported her towards the pub's entrance.

'I'll get you up to a room'

'But what about questionin' the locals?'

'I'll get you settled, and then I'll take a poster down to the bar and ask around. I'll order some room service while I'm down there, while you relax. You're bushed.'

Beth nodded. 'You're right. I'm just so worried. I know we're close to findin' Maureen, but will Harrison be with her when we do? No one's seen him. How do we know she hasn't harmed him?'

Ron wrapped his arms around her, kissed her forehead and rocked her gently. 'She's no reason to harm him. She loves him. That's what this is all about… she wants to keep him to herself. She may be irrational, deluded even, but I can't believe she'd hurt him. You and me, probably, but not Harrison.'

Beth leaned against Ron as he led her into the pub, booked a room and guided her upstairs. Their room was small, furnished only with a double bed, wardrobe and a second door that presumably led to the en-suite. Simple, but clean. She collapsed onto the bed, which was soft and comfortable, and leaned back against the pillows while Ron lifted her legs onto the bed, slipped off her shoes and rubbed her feet.

'I'll be back in a few minutes. You just rest.'

'Thanks,' she murmured, as she drifted off to sleep.

# Chapter Thirty

Beth glanced through the menu. 'I'm really not hungry.'

'You need to eat some breakfast. You hardly had anything yesterday.'

'The thought of food makes me feel sick.'

Ron reached across the table and took her hand. 'Come on, darling. It'll be light enough to start searching again soon. I'm sure we're close to finding Harrison now. I don't want to be worrying about you fainting in the process.'

The young waitress appeared at their side.

Beth sighed. 'Coffee and scrambled egg with brown toast please.'

'And I'll also take coffee, with a full English, please.'

The girl scurried away.

'I'm still worried about why Maureen's been seen, but not Harrison.'

'Don't be. We'll find them both anytime soon now. I promise.'

Beth's eyes filled with tears. 'I hope you're right. I can't take this not knowin'.'

She looked around the small dining room of the inn: the walls were painted a very pale blue; the six tables had cream pedestals and polished oak tops with matching chairs; the tablemats were turquoise, as were the curtains and cushions, with a dark blue carpet.

Ron followed her gaze. 'Do you like the colour scheme? We could use it in our new home, perhaps?'

Beth stood quickly and crossed the room. She understood what he was trying to do. He was trying so hard, but seriously, she couldn't think about bleddy colour schemes right now. Not until she knew that Harrison was okay.

She looked out of the window. It was getting lighter, but she supposed he was right about waiting a few more minutes. She wandered back, glancing at the pictures on the wall. She stopped before a small oil painting and gazed vacantly at the beach scene. Wait. Her eyes fixed on the painting. Her pulse quickened. Could it be? She peered closer.

'Oh my God. Look, Ron...come and see this.'

Ron raced to her side. 'What is it?'

'It's the cove in the photograph Maureen showed me.'

'Are you sure? Those coves all look a bit alike to me.'

'I'm sure. See these rocks here...' She pointed to a pile of fallen rocks and a cliff on the right-hand side of the beach. 'It reminded me of a slumberin' giant. Look, here's his legs, his body, and this bit is his head, slumped down on his chest.'

Ron frowned as he studied the picture. 'I always knew you had a good imagination.'

The waitress returned with a pot of coffee and a jug of milk and placed them on their table.

Beth rushed to her side and grabbed her arm. 'Do you know where this cove is?'

'It's known locally as Kayak Cove. It's a couple of miles from here.'

'Kayak Cove! That's it. How do we get there?'

'Turn right as you leave by the main entrance... towards St Piran...drive for about two miles and look out for the sign on your right. It points you down a track that leads to the car park.'

'Thanks.' Beth grabbed Ron's hand. 'Come on, let's go.'

'But you need to eat.'

'Your breakfasts are ready now,' the waitress said. 'I'll fetch them.'

'Okay, compromise,' Ron said. 'Make them into sandwiches. We'll eat as we drive.'


Ron parked the car.

Beth jumped out and ran towards the beach. 'Come on, Ron.'

Ron followed close behind her. They reached the sand dunes and stopped when they got to the top.

'Look,' Beth pointed. 'A café. Perhaps they've seen them.'

They raced towards the proprietor, who was putting out tables and chairs. Beth showed him a poster.

'Have you seen this boy? He'd probably be with an older woman who he calls, Nana Mo.'

He looked at the picture and scratched his head. 'There was a young lad here yesterday, caused a bit of a kafuffle. He'd wandered away from his grandmother. A customer here bought him an ice cream and sat with him until she showed up. The two women exchanged a few words. My customer accused the other woman of being irresponsible, which didn't go down too well.'

'And was it this boy?'

'It looks like him.'

Beth's heart rate increased. At last. Their first proof that Harrison was still alive.

'Or at least, it could have been.' He squinted back at the picture and frowned. 'They all look the same at that age.'

Beth felt as though she'd been kicked in the stomach. 'But you said it was him?'

He shrugged. 'Could be.'

Beth and Ron thanked him and walked onto the beach holding hands.

Beth sighed. 'Where do we go from here?'

'Let's go to the end of the beach and explore those rocks, see if we can enlist the support of your slumbering giant.'

As they neared the rocks, Beth could feel the excitement building. She ran the last few yards and then turned to face Ron.

'This is definitely the spot where the photograph was taken. It must have been them yesterday. Look, here's a sandcastle that's been kicked over. I can just see Harrison building that. And there's a footpath to St Piran. Shall we try it?'

'Let's go back and fetch the car. We can drive through the village and look for the Morris. It'll be quicker.'

Beth didn't want to go backwards, she wanted to push on, but Ron was right of course. And they might need the car. Especially if Maureen tried to do a runner. She turned back towards the carpark and could've sworn she caught a scent of Harrison on the sea breeze.

'Hold on, Harrison,' she whispered. 'We're nearly there. Please, just hold on a little while longer.'

# Chapter Thirty-one

Maureen jumped as someone knocked on the front door. Her heart pounded as she ran to the lounge. Was it that woman from the beach café yesterday? Perhaps Maureen's attempt to make her believe they lived a long drive away hadn't worked? Had she come looking for them or, even worse, had she reported them to the police? She made sure she was hidden by the curtain and peeped through the window, then sighed with relief as she spotted the delivery van in the drive.

'Coming!' she called out, before entering the kitchen where Harrison was eating his bowl of cereals.

'Stay there. Remember what I told you. We are in hiding from that big brown bear. Stay here quietly and I'll bring you a treat.'

Harrison carried on eating his cereals while she picked up her purse and went to the front door. 'Thanks for waiting, I was just fetching my purse.'

'That's okay. Would you like me to carry this through to the kitchen for you? It's quite heavy.'

'No!'

Maureen looked at the man's surprised expression. She hadn't meant for that to come out so sharply, but she didn't want him recognising Harrison from the TV appeal. Her picture had been an old one and she doubted anyone would recognise her from it, but a missing small boy was not something anyone could easily forget.

'I'm sorry, would you just put it down here? How much do I owe you?'

'With delivery charges, that will be thirty-two pounds please.'

Maureen paid the money and closed the door behind him. She bent down to pick up the box, grunting as she carried it through to the kitchen table.

'Have you finished your cereals, Harrison?'

'Finished,' Harrison held up his empty bowl.

'Good boy. Do you need a wee before we go for our morning walk?'

Harrison shook his head. 'Can we look for the bear in the woods?'

'As long as he doesn't catch us. Can you run fast?'

Harrison nodded. *'We're going on a bear hunt,'* he sang. He got down from the table and began to dance. *'We're not scared.'* He put his hands up in front of his chest, like paws, and roared.

Maureen laughed. 'Alright, we'll go as soon as that van driver goes. Is he still here? I didn't hear him pull away.' She returned to the lounge and looked out. The van was still on the driveway. 'What *is* he doing?'

Maureen grabbed her coat, changed her slippers for her boots and helped Harrison into his.

'Wait here, Harrison. I'll find out what he's up to.'

Maureen walked up to the driver's window, which was open. The delivery man had his arm resting on the door and was eating a pasty. They were trapped. This was the one problem with the cottage: there was a front door onto the drive, and a side door from the kitchen that was also visible from the drive; there was no way for her and Harrison to leave unseen, not while that silly man was sitting out there.

'What do you think you're doing?' she asked crossly.

'Eating my breakfast. I had an early start this morning. Missed out.'

'Well, that's not my problem, young man. Go and eat your pasty somewhere else.'

The man pushed his half-eaten pasty into the paper bag he'd been using to catch the crumbs. He threw it onto the passenger seat, started his engine and pulled away. Maureen watched his van disappearing up the drive in a flurry of dust. She sighed, turned back to the front door and pushed it open.

'Come on, Harrison. Let's get going on that bear hunt.'

Maureen locked the door behind them and then steered Harrison onto the footpath. Harrison ran in front of her, picked up a stick and poked it into a small hole under a tree.

'A rabbit lives here.'

'Are you sure? It doesn't look big enough for a rabbit, more like a mouse.'

'It's a small rabbit.'

'It would need to be.' Maureen smiled at him.

'It ate a mushroom and got small.'

'Like in *Alice in Wonderland*.'

Harrison nodded.

They walked to the end of the footpath and stepped onto the sandy beach. Maureen noticed a woman wearing a red anorak walking towards them and realised it was the same woman from their encounter yesterday. The last thing she wanted was to bump into her.

'Can we do sandcastles?' Harrison asked.

'Not today. No beach today. We'll go somewhere different. Let's go this way and walk along the cliff path.'

# Chapter Thirty-two

Ron drove slowly. Beth forced herself to remain silent when she desperately wanted to shout at him to hurry up. She knew they needed to be thorough, but this was excruciating. They peered out through the windows, checking both sides of the road as they got closer to the village.

'Holy Cow! Stupid idiot!' Ron shouted as a white van pulled out from a driveway that was partially obscured by some roadside bushes. The van screeched to a halt, grazing Ron's bumper as it stopped. A young man jumped out and ran to Ron's window.

'I'm so sorry,' he gushed. 'I was blinded by the sun. It's so low at the moment. I simply didn't see you. Are you all right?'

Ron looked across at Beth who was loosening her seat belt. 'Are you okay, darling?'

Beth nodded.

'Thank goodness you're not hurt.' The young man stood back from the car to allow Ron space to climb out. 'My boss is going to kill me as it is.'

Ron clambered from his car and inspected his front bumper. 'No harm done, mate. Just be a bit more careful next time.'

'I was probably a bit distracted to be honest. Some old woman just gave me an earful. I delivered her groceries and then sat on her drive eating my breakfast pasty. I tried to explain I'd had an early start this morning. Can't see what harm I was doing or why she got so uppity, acting as though she owned the place.'

'Doesn't she?' Ron asked.

'That cottage is only a rental. I deliver there a lot in the summer.'

'Was there a young boy at the house?' Beth asked.

'I didn't see anyone, but then she wouldn't let me carry the groceries in like I normally do. Anyway, I'll be off now, lots more deliveries to make.' He waved goodbye, got back in his van and drove away.

'Come on, let's check it out.' Beth said.

Ron nodded. 'You bet!' He started the car and pulled into the dirt track.

They drove for a few hundred yards until they saw a small granite cottage.

Beth sighed. 'No sign of the Morris.'

'I'll just have a check of the garage.' Ron pointed and climbed out of the car. He peered through the garage window. 'It's here! Come and look.' He beckoned Beth over.

She raced to his side, stood on her tip-toes and looked. It was quite dark and gloomy inside, but the outline of the Morris Minor Traveller was unmistakable. Adrenalin surged through Beth as she ran to the front step and hammered her fists on the wooden door.

'Maureen, open this door!' Beth tried turning the doorknob but the door was locked. 'At once, do you hear?'

Her efforts were met with silence.

Ron banged his fist on the unopened door. 'Mrs James?'

Beth ran to the side of the house. 'Look. There's a side door here.' She tried the handle. 'Locked. Come on Ron, she could be in there hiding.'

Ron joined her. 'Stand back,' he said as he lunged against the door with his shoulder.

The door crashed open.

'I'll take upstairs, you take down,' he said.

Beth raced around the kitchen, flinging open the pantry and cupboard doors, then searched the downstairs toilet, lounge and hall. Nothing.

Ron ran down the stairs to join her. 'Nothing up there, although, I did find this.'

He pushed Harrison's blue rabbit into her outstretched hands.

She sniffed the soft fur. 'Oh, Harrison. Where are you?'

'She can't have gone far. The delivery van only left a few minutes ago. I'll get hold of Nicky. We need the police over here, now.'

Ron spoke to Nicky and gave her details of where they were as Beth quickly searched the back garden and outbuildings.

Returning to the front drive, Beth waited while Ron finished his call to Nicky. Her eyes were drawn to a gap in the hedge that led onto a narrow pathway that ran along by the side of the cottage. She walked over to examine it and discovered a small wooden arrow nailed to a tree.

'Ron, there's a footpath here. Looks like it goes down, through the woods to the beach.'

Ron joined her and they began to walk along the path. 'Nicky says one patrol car is going to the car park, where we were earlier, and another two are on their way to another one about a mile west of here on the coastal path. If we walk straight on then we'll have a sort of pincher movement going on. We'll get him back. She can't get away this time.'

Beth ran ahead, turned and beckoned to Ron. 'Come on. We can't be far behind them. Hurry up.'

'They may not have stuck to the path. Remember, Harrison likes to explore. I don't want to miss them by going too fast.'

Beth sighed. 'I expect you're right. I just want to catch up with them. I'm desperate to have him in my arms, smother him in kisses and tell him everythin's goin' to be alright.' She walked along the path, looking from right to left, listening, in the hope that she would hear Harrison shouting or laughing. But the only sound was the wind rustling through the trees and their feet crunching through the leaf litter.

Ten minutes later, the trees thinned and the footpath forked. One signpost pointed straight on and was inscribed: *to the beach*. The other: *coastal path*. They ignored the stile and two minutes later stepped onto the beach.

'We're back to my slumberin' giant.' Beth pointed. 'Look. There's Maureen.' Beth ran onto the soft sand and raced towards a woman walking along the shoreline. 'Maureen!'

Something wasn't right; this woman was younger than Maureen, and where was Harrison? Her feet slipped in the soft sand and she fell to her knees, scuffing up sand that blew into her face as she hurried to her feet. 'Please stop?' she shouted as she recovered her balance and began to run again, brushing aside the gritty tears that stung her cheeks.

The woman turned and waited for Beth to catch up. 'Can I help you?'

'We're looking for our son, Harrison.' Beth pulled a crumpled poster from the back pocket of her jeans and smoothed it flat. 'He's three. He'd be with an older woman called Maureen James. He calls her Nana Mo. Have you seen him?'

'I believe I have. Yesterday. They were here on the beach. I tell you, my dear, you should not trust that stupid woman to look after a young child. I'm sorry if it's your mother or something, but she was so careless, falling asleep like that, leaving him to wander off. He could have been drowned. Or kidnapped. I gave her a piece of my mind, I can tell you.'

Ron joined them.

'Ron, this lady saw Harrison yesterday. Oh, thank goodness, he's still alive.'

'I saw them again, only a few minutes ago. They came out from that footpath over there, but when she spotted me, they turned around and went onto the coastal footpath.' She pointed to where the village footpath joined the beach. 'Over the stile back there.'

Beth felt a surge of adrenalin as she turned and raced back across the beach.

'Thanks,' Ron shouted over his shoulder to the woman as he chased after Beth. He caught up with her just before she reached the stile. 'Wait. Before we go after them, we'd better let the police know where they are.' He pulled out his mobile, rang Nicky and gave her an update. She promised to get a message to the patrol cars. 'Right...now we can go.'

# Chapter Thirty-three

Maureen looked out to sea. The sun was shining through the clouds. Shafts of light broke through and reflected on the water below them, reminding her of a biblical painting. Any minute now, she expected a dove to arrive, probably holding an olive twig. Instead, three seagulls appeared and circled above them before swooping down and plunging into the waves.

'Look, Harrison. The seagulls are fishing.'

'I cold.' He shivered and stuffed his free hand into his pocket. 'Want to go home now.'

'Just a bit further. Come on. If we walk faster, we'll get warm.' She dragged him along the path. Where on earth was she going? Harrison's little legs would be giving out any time now, and that clamber up to the clifftop had made her sciatica far worse. Excruciating. The thought of a log fire and a pot of tea seemed very inviting. She paused and turned to see if the woman in the red anorak was coming after them. She saw no one.

'Okay, Harrison, let's stand here for a while and get our breath back.'

'Want to go home.'

'In a minute. First, let's see if the seagulls are still fishing.'

The original three seagulls had been joined by four others. They all sat on the water, bobbing like corks on the waves, which appeared to be getting bigger. Some were now topped with little foaming crests, which curled over and scurried towards the rocks below them. She'd never seen it look quite as rough as this on her earlier walks. She and Giles used to love walking parts of the Coastal Path when they'd first come to Cornwall. They were both eager to explore. Pregnancy, and then Anna's arrival, made the walking difficult, but they'd promised themselves that when he retired, they would attempt the entire path, all two-hundred-and-fifty-odd miles of it. How could life be so cruel?

Her relationship with Giles and her faith in God had been destroyed the moment she'd discovered Giles's infidelity. She'd been so full of rage and had even considered smothering him, but the thought of being charged with murder and the consequences for Anna had reined in her hatred. She could easily have given him an overdose and claimed he took it himself, but she couldn't risk the loss of his life insurance, which she knew didn't pay out for suicide. For those last few weeks, she'd found it impossible to look at him. In the end, it had been a relief when he'd died.

She clutched Harrison's hand. Surely, that nosey woman would have gone by now. She turned around and gasped.

'What's the matter, Nana Mo?'

'Nothing, sweetie. We have to go. Come on, quickly.'

Maureen dragged Harrison along the footpath.

How had they found her? What could she do? There was no way she could outrun them, especially not with Harrison hanging back like this. Time for a re-think.

# Chapter Thirty-four

Ron held Beth's hand and pulled her up the steep path.

'How on earth did she manage to get up here?' Beth's trainers slipped on the small pebbles.

'You can do anything when you're desperate. She probably thought that woman was about to report her. We're nearly at the top of this steep bit. The path levels off to a gentle slope here.'

Beth stood to catch her breath, held her hand up to shield the sun from her eyes and searched the landscape in front of them. 'There they are. Look.' She pointed.

They ran across the field. Beth's pulse raced as they got closer. It was Maureen, and Harrison was with her. Thank God!

Maureen glanced over her shoulder and quickened her pace. She was practically dragging Harrison. Beth could hear him crying, poor little mite. How could she be so cruel? She must know there's nowhere else to hide.

Maureen stopped suddenly in her tracks. Two police officers, one in uniform and one in plain clothes, walked towards Maureen from the opposite side of the field. The man in plain clothes looked vaguely familiar. Beth glanced over her shoulder and spotted two further uniformed officers quickly catching them up. She sighed with relief.

'Mummy!'

The tremble in Harrison's voice pierced Beth's heart. She wanted to rush to his side but Ron held her arm.

'Wait Beth. They know what they're doing. Let them handle it.'

'But I want to go to him.'

'I know, but we don't want her thinking she's trapped.'

The two uniformed officers caught up with them. One bent over and struggled to catch his breath, while the younger one spoke.

'Don't go any closer. We'll wait here with you, but we need to give DCI Sweeny space to negotiate with Mrs James.'

Beth glanced towards the cliff edge. Of course, she recognised him now. No wonder he looked familiar.

Maureen had backed towards the cliff edge and was still gripping Harrison's hand.

Beth grabbed Ron's arm. 'She won't hurt him, will she? Please tell me she won't.'

Ron pulled her close and hugged her.

Maureen watched the plainclothes policeman edge closer.

'Come on now, Mrs James,' DCI Sweeny said.

'Don't come any nearer or I swear I'll jump.'

'I'll stay here, don't worry. I won't come any closer. Now then, what's all this about? Why don't you come away from the edge and let's talk this through?'

'I'm staying here. We are staying here, aren't we Harrison?'

'I want my mummy.'

'She's not having him. She doesn't deserve him. She was going to move in with that Steve and take him away from me. I had to stop her.'

'You stopped her?'

Maureen smiled. 'You didn't think I had it in me, did you?'

'I'm sure it was self-defence. Did he attack you?'

'He wanted to ruin my life by taking Harrison away from me. In the same way Tony took my daughter and baby grandson away from me. I made sure he suffered too.'

'Mrs James...don't worry about that now. Let's concentrate on getting you and Harrison back home.' DCI Sweeney reached out his hand towards her.

Maureen realised there was no way back from this. Not only would she lose Harrison, but she would also lose her freedom and spend the rest of her life locked away. She'd rather be dead. She clutched Harrison tighter and took another step back towards the edge of the cliff. She glanced over her shoulder and could see the rocks below. The waves were swirling over them, creating whirlpools and froth. Her head spun. She swayed.

Beth watched in horror as Maureen teetered on the edge of the cliff, swaying in the breeze. Her heart thudded in her chest, drowning out the sound of the waves as they crashed onto the rocks below.

'Harrison!' Beth screamed. 'Let him go! Don't hurt him!'

'Mummy!' Harrison sobbed.

Maureen pulled Harrison close in front of her and glanced over her shoulder once more.

'Come now, Mrs James. We don't want anyone getting hurt here, do we?' DCI Sweeney's voice sounded desperate.

Maureen laughed. 'They don't deserve him. And if I can't have him, neither will they.'

She took another step back, pulling Harrison with her. She was only inches away from the cliff edge now.

Pain shot across Beth's forehead as her pulse raced. Any second now, the ground would give way and Harrison would plunge to his death. She had to do something to save him, but what? 'Harrison!' She screamed. 'Stranger Danger!'

Harrison turned around and kicked Maureen on her shins. She let go of him as she wobbled on the cliff edge, her arms flapping. Harrison raced towards Beth, who knelt as he threw himself into her arms. Ron fell to his knees beside them both and wrapped his arms around them.

'My baby...' Beth rocked Harrison while tears poured down her cheeks. She looked up through tear filled eyes and glanced over to the clifftop, but Maureen had gone.

'Where's Nana Mo?' Harrison looked back towards the cliffs. 'Please, Mummy, I say sorry I kick her. It was an accident.'

Ron knelt down and took hold of his hand. 'Don't worry, buddy. Nana Mo wanted to take you away from Mummy and Daddy. You did the right thing.'

'Was she naughty?'

Ron nodded.

'Will the police take her away and lock her up in prison. Like Paddington?'

'A bit like that,' Ron said. 'The same principle anyway.'

'Will Prince Ipul look after Nana Mo?'

'I'm sure he will.' Ron ruffled his hair.

A helicopter surged over their heads and hovered above the cliff. A man appeared at the open hatchway and was slowly winched down below the cliff edge, out of sight.

DCI Sweeny walked over to join them. 'I think you should get out of here now, while we secure the crime scene.'

'Crime scene. What do you mean? What crime?'

'Why don't you take Harrison home? I'll be in touch as soon as we know what's what.'

Ron gripped her arm. 'Come on, darling. Let's get off.'

Beth wondered if there was any chance that Maureen could have survived the fall. She doubted it.

How were they ever going to explain to Harrison that Nana Mo was dead, and even worse, that it was because he'd kicked her. Is that what they meant by *crime scene*. Surely the police wouldn't take any action against Harrison. He'd only kicked Maureen because he thought it was a game. Thinking about it, she'd been the one who'd called out. Perhaps she would get the blame for Maureen's death? She was only on parole. Would she be whisked back to jail?

She wrapped her arms around Harrison and kissed the top of his head. She couldn't cope with the thought that, now she had Harrison and Ron back, she was about to lose them both all over again.

Ron picked Harrison up and swung him onto his shoulders. 'Let's get you home, buddy.' He paused and frowned. 'Although, that's a thought, where is home now?'

# Chapter Thirty-five

Beth walked down the path, past the beds of lush green ferns and shrubs. A small hummingbird hovered as it collected nectar from a large trumpet-like flower. She breathed deeply and the aroma of essential oils that pervaded the spa resort mingled with the smell of the natural perfume from the various plants. The effect was so soothing she couldn't help but smile.

Beth wiggled her toes into the white powdery sand and gazed out across the turquoise sea. That day on the clifftop seemed a long way away now, although it had only been seven months. On Nicky's advice, she and Ron had returned to the Blue Lion and waited for DCI Sweeny to arrive. They'd been fortunate and changed their booking to a family room, which meant they could eat lunch in private, and then Harrison had been able to snuggle down for an afternoon nap clutching his fluffy blue rabbit. DCI Sweeny had turned up mid-afternoon.

Beth, by that time, had convinced herself that he was there to arrest her for the death of Maureen. They'd already checked on Facebook and read that an elderly woman had died following a fall from the cliffs.

He'd quickly reassured her. It was a tragic accident as far as they were concerned, and Maureen's clifftop 'confession' to the murder of Tony and Steve would ensure that Beth would be exonerated. He had also advised her to talk to her solicitor about applying for compensation for wrongful imprisonment. He had told her that the Justice Secretary had the discretion to pay compensation to a wrongfully convicted person when new facts proved, beyond reasonable doubt, that the person imprisoned had been innocent of the offence and that there had been a miscarriage of justice. Neil had made an application under something called Section 133 and an independent assessor awarded her £200,000.

Ron had refused to have any say in how the money should be spent. He'd argued that she was the one who had suffered, and she alone should decide. In the end, they'd agreed to spend some of it on upgrading their new home in Goldenbank to a larger, four-bedroomed property, and some on a family holiday to St. Lucia. There'd still be enough left to upgrade the car, buy a puppy for Harrison and have some savings. It was amazing to think that their family was now financially secure as a result of Maureen's grief for her dead grandson and her misguided and obsessional belief that Harrison was, in some way, her compensation. It was also comforting to know that Harrison's future was financially secure, thanks to Maureen's will. The house had been sold and the money invested in a Trust Fund until he reached the age of twenty-one.

Beth walked further onto the sands, towards the pavilion where Ron and Harrison were waiting for her. Harrison looked so cute in his new suit, white shirt and blue silk tie that matched his father's outfit.

Ron turned to watch her approach and smiled encouragingly. She gripped the small bunch of white fuchsia that had been delivered to her that morning, freshly picked from the hotel grounds. Her long white muslin dress, the coronet of small white roses on her head and her bare feet made her feel like a free spirit. Free to retake her wedding vows. This part of the holiday had been Ron's suggestion, but one to which she'd been happy to agree.

Harrison stood next to Ron, a small velvet cushion held in his hands. On it was the diamond eternity ring that Ron had chosen for her. Ron grinned from ear to ear as she drew level with them both and then took a step to his right, giving her space to stand between them.

'You look lovely,' Ron smiled.

'Like a princess,' Harrison said.

The registrar moved forward and stood before them. 'Ron and Beth, we are here today to renew your wedding vows. I will ask each of you, in turn, to make your vow, starting with you, Ron.'

Ron turned to face Beth and took her left hand in his. 'Beth, in the past I have done things I'm not proud of. I abandoned you with our small baby son, while I went off to volunteer for humanitarian relief work in troubled places. I should have shown you more understanding, protected you, and prevented you from falling into the nightmare you have endured. I was wrong. I hope you will forgive me. I am here today to pledge that you, and our children, will always be my priority. I will always be there for you, no matter what life brings our way. I vow to give you all that I am and all that I have for the rest of our lives. This is my solemn promise.'

Beth's eyes brimmed with happy tears. 'Ron, you have supported me through the best, and the worst moments of my life. There is nothin' to forgive. Neither of us truly understood what we had, until we foolishly almost lost it. I will spend the rest of my life makin' sure that you always feel appreciated and loved. I will also abstain from alcohol for the rest of my life. This is my solemn promise.'

Ron picked the eternity ring up from the cushion and slipped it onto Beth's finger.

'You may now kiss your wife,' the registrar said.

Ron kissed Beth tenderly, while Harrison jumped up and down beside them.

'Me too!' he shouted.

Beth bent down and kissed him. She forced herself to restrain from sweeping him up into her arms and swinging him around, the way he liked. That would have to wait for a while. She patted her tummy, where the slightest of bulges was only just apparent. Four months from now they would be in their new home, with a puppy *and* a sister for Harrison.

She wasn't quite sure which he was the most excited about.

# Acknowledgements

I offer my heartfelt thanks to my husband, Harold; our daughter, Rachael, her husband, Dan, and our two adorable grandsons, Hector and Arthur. Without their love and encouragement, this book would never have been completed.

I am also indebted to Elaine Singer, my fellow beta-reader.

My thanks go to Ed Handyside at Cornerstones, and to Kath Morgan who's editing and insightful comments helped to polish the final draft.

In addition, I would like to thank Ken Allen, Mary Cooper, Maureen Woodhouse and Peter Woodford, who spent many hours proof reading the manuscript.

And finally, a really big thank you to Charlotte Mouncey of Bookstyle, who created, yet another, amazing cover design for me.

Thank you, one and all. X.

9 781839 756900